THE RULES OF MISTLETOE

TAYLOR EPPERSON

Happy Reading!

TayEpp ♡

The Rules of Mistletoe

Copyright © 2023 by Taylor Epperson

https://authortaylorepperson.com/
Sign up for Taylor Epperson's Newsletter

Cover Design Emily Wittig Designs

Editor: Kristen Hamilton, Kristen's Red Pen, http://kristensredpen.com/

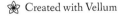 Created with Vellum

For my parents, grandparents, aunts & uncles, and all of my cousins. Thank you for making Christmas (and my childhood) so incredibly magical.

 *chapter 1*

HOLLY

Rule #9: My future husband and I will have a meet-cute. We'll actually like each other right from the start, not like in Harry Met Sally

BEING in a crowded room and feeling like I am completely alone feels like the story of my life. But it never feels more true than when I am at a faculty party. I stand on the edges of the decorated gymnasium, watching my co-workers and their partners mingle and laugh. "Jingle Bell Rock" is playing faintly in the background, loud enough for us to hear the music, but not loud enough that you can't have a conversation—not that I'm having any conversations.

I glance around again, looking for someone to talk to. I might feel a bit lonely, but there's also a part of me that's bursting right now because Christmas is one week away. In two days I'll be headed home to see my family, and nothing is better than Christmas with my family. The excitement inside of me is about to boil over. I need to talk to someone—anyone—about how much I love this holiday. But it probably won't gain me any good graces with my co-workers. Though no one has actually said it to my face, I know I've been dubbed as the quirky, weird art teacher. And that's okay, because that's exactly who I am. I wear bright, funky clothes and sometimes I randomly sing instructions to my students.

"Stop looking like you're all sad and alone," Adrienne, my roommate and coworker, says as she walks up next to me. "I know you're thrilled to be here because of Christmas, but you aren't talking to anyone."

"Maybe it's the other people not talking to me that's the problem." I smile at her. "See, now I don't look so sad and alone, you're talking to me."

"She lives with you, she doesn't count," Felix—Adrienne's cousin—says; he came with her as her plus one and it's good to see him again. I didn't have anyone to bring because all of the people I know in California are here in this room. I have lived here for three years, and I've yet to meet someone who doesn't work at the school, or is related to someone who works at the school.

"She totally counts." I give both of them a hug. "And I am glad you two finally showed up, so I don't have to stand here all awkward and alone."

Adrienne glances around the room. She teaches ninth grade English at our high school. "You could have talked to Mr. Sullivan."

I hate how she waggles her eyebrows as she says his name. It makes it feel like the unrequited feelings I have for our boss are childish and juvenile. I give her a light shove, careful not to spill my cup of hot chocolate—with extra candy canes in it, because that makes it taste even more like Christmas. Felix snorts.

"Do you have something to say?" I whirl at him and he holds up his hands innocently.

"Sweetie," Adrienne loops one of her arms through mine. I've never been a huge fan of physical affection; words of affirmation are more my thing if we're getting technical about it. But Adrienne's touch always seems to bring me some level of comfort. "You're nearly thirty. He's almost forty. Talk to him, not as your boss. Actually, talk to him. See where things go."

Just at the thought of it, my hands get clammy. Deep down, I know I'm being slightly ridiculous. How can I be about to turn twenty-nine and still not have the nerve to talk to a man that I'm attracted to? A man that follows every single rule and dream I have for my ideal husband. He's everything I've ever wanted, everything I've ever dreamed of.

Which is exactly why I can't talk to him.

My mom showed me my first romantic comedy—*While You Were Sleeping*—when I was just six years old. I've been hooked on all the classics ever since. I've been dreaming about finding a love like they do in all of the movies since I was seven.

When I was fifteen, my mom had me and my sister make a list of rules for our dream guy for fun. I'm pretty sure my sister Tally lost hers shortly after that, because she'd only been about ten at the time, but I've kept mine. I knew what I wanted then, and it is still what I want now.

Adrienne thinks I need to dump my list and just casually date, see what's out there. I can't though. It's important to me to find someone who follows all of my rules. And Mr. Sullivan follows all of them.

But the idea of actually talking to Jim—Mr. Sullivan I mean—almost makes me break out in hives. Just like always though, my eyes dart to where Jim stands in the middle of the room, laughing at something that Mr. Jones, the PE teacher, is saying. No matter where we are, I can always pick him out in a crowd. Knowing where Jim is and what he's doing seems as easy to me as breathing right now. A fact that I've never told anyone, because I know that's probably borderline stalkerish.

I should also really start calling him Mr. Sullivan in my head, maybe that would help me squash my feelings and help me have a half decent conversation with him.

"I can wave him over here," Adrienne says, lifting her hand. I tug it back down.

"No!"

"You've got to do it sometime, little chicka." Felix pinches my arm affectionately. He's the only person allowed to call me that, and it's only because I am little. I'm barely five feet tall, not that I really notice I'm that short, except for when I'm around extremely tall people. Like Drew Rossi, the other art teacher.

I blink in surprise. I don't think about Drew that often, but I am thinking about his tall, broad frame now because he's just walked through the doors of the gym, his hands stuffed in his pockets, jaw tight. "What's he doing here?"

Adrienne and Felix both turn to see Drew standing in the doorway. "Mr. Anti-social decided to make an appearance."

I nod in response to Adrienne's words, truly wondering why he's here. I take in his tall, built frame, slightly matted hair—probably from his bike helmet—and dark beard. He's wearing a forest green sweater, so at least he kind of looks like Christmas. But in the three years that I've lived in California and taught here in Laguna Beach, I've never seen Drew at a social event. And our school hosts them often for teachers—something about wanting to build comradery. Drew doesn't do social events. It is a well-known fact that he isn't a people person. He doesn't have friends or people—something I quickly found out after I moved in and invited him to one of Adrienne's movie nights. It felt like the right thing to do, since he lives in the little beach cottage next door and he is the only other person in the art department, but he shut it down fast, saying he doesn't do friends.

Ever since then, I try to be my bubbly, charming self whenever I'm around him just to see if I can make his frown deepen. I usually win this weird bet I've made with myself. At this point though, I'm fairly certain that there's nothing in this world that could make Drew Rossi smile. The kids love him though, and I haven't figured out why.

I take a sip of my hot chocolate, the only thing right now that will help me not soak in all his grumpiness. Because even though I am generally successful at making him frown more, his bad attitude around me always seems to bring me down. The pepperminty chocolate gives me a burst of energy.

"You know what, maybe I will talk to Jim." I pull my arm out from Adrienne's who is now gaping at me.

"Really?" She sounds surprised. I'm surprised, honestly. But maybe it's time to be brave. I walk away from her and Felix before I can change my mind. It's only when I'm almost to Jim— Mr. Sullivan I mean—that I notice I'm not the only one walking toward him.

Drew reaches him right before I do, giving me a look that says 'what are you doing?' and what am I doing exactly? But it's obvious where I'm headed, so I can't back down now. Instead, I make my smile bigger as I reach the two men who are now talking to each other.

"Hello!" I say a tad bit too cheerfully and both of them pause their conversation and look down at me. They literally have to look down because they both are over six feet tall.

"Hello," Drew says with what some people might think is a smirk, but it's really just less of a frown than the normal expression he has on his face. But I won't let him or his grumpiness derail me. I give him a tiny nod in response and look up at Jim.

"Hi," he greets, his tone telling me he's surprised that I've approached him in a setting that isn't a school meeting, which is the only place I've ever actually spoken to him. "Are you enjoying the party, Ms. Nelson?"

I hate that he doesn't call me Holly, but he's talking to me and I haven't passed out yet. I can do this. "Yes! Christmas is my favorite holiday, so I love any extra parties to celebrate it."

I swear Drew lets out a snort, but he covers it up with a cough. "Excuse me," he says, "I need a drink, I'll be back."

Then he's gone, and it's just me and Mr. Jim Sullivan. He's so tall that I have to crane my neck to really look into his deep brown eyes. His sandy blonde hair is cut short and there's not even a hint of a five o'clock shadow—which I love because I imagine beards would make kissing scratchy.

I shift nervously on my feet. Now is *not* the time to be thinking about kissing. At all. Period. Or to be thinking about the fact that I've never actually kissed anyone before or no one has ever kissed me. I mean, there have been moments and dates when men have tried, but it wasn't the perfect time—I mean, come on, how romantic is getting kissed in front of your door? It's so cliché. I want something better. But because of that, it means I'm less than a week away from turning twenty-nine and I've never been kissed.

"No mistletoe?" I blurt out of nowhere and Jim looks more surprised than before. "I mean, it just seems like a very festive thing to have at a work party."

I really need to stop talking before I say anything else that will embarrass myself. But I can't seem to make my mouth stop moving. "Not that I've ever kissed anyone under mistletoe before."

Oh my gosh, Holly. SHUT UP. This man does not need to know about your kissing history. Seriously, why can I not stop thinking about my kissing history? Or lack of history.

"Anyway." Now the words seem to be pouring out of my

mouth like I have no control over them—which to be fair, I don't think I do. "Are you going home for Christmas?"

Jim is still watching me with an amused look on his face and I know I've completely messed this all up. There is no way this man sees me as more than a young, nervous teacher. What is it about him that makes me want to say anything and everything that comes to mind without pausing for a break and makes me sound like a complete fool?

"I am. Home to Minnesota." He shivers, as if the thought of going to the Midwest this time of year is the worst idea possible. "I tried to get my parents to come and visit me, but they said they don't like to travel in the snow."

I laugh. "But you have to travel in the snow to get to them?"

"Yes." Jim smiles like he's reliving a happy memory. "But it's worth it. My sister and her family live there too, and I love being with all of them."

I nearly let out a sigh. Do not fall in love with him more, do not. But he does fit rule number eight which is all about having a good relationship with his family.

"That's fun though, even if it's snowy," I say. "I'm going home too. To Utah, which will probably have snow, but I don't think it's as cold as Minnesota."

"I've never seen snow," Drew says out of nowhere, and Jim and I both glance at him. I didn't even realize he'd come back. When Jim's around, it's like the only thing I can focus on is him.

"Man, we have got to change that," Jim says and I feel a funny tickle run through my body. Drew, the man who has no friends is friends with Jim? "Are you sure you don't want to come home with me for Christmas? The offer still stands."

Drew glances in my direction then back to Jim. "No, thank you though. I've got other plans."

Yeah, his plans probably include hibernating in his little beach cottage all alone and running in the morning like he does every day. Not that I notice much, I'm generally a heavy, late sleeper. But if I'm working on a painting, it's like sleep doesn't exist so I've seen him out in the mornings off to run on the beach. What kind of crazy person wakes up at the crack of dawn to go running? I will never understand that. But I'd bet his plans include lots of running. And whatever it is he does in his beach cottage. Bungalow. Whatever.

"What did you say you were doing again?" Jim asks Drew, and I'm glad because I was going to make a bigger fool of myself by asking that question.

"I'm going home with a friend," Drew says, looking at me again and I take a small step back. Why does he keep looking at me like that when he says friend? Like I'm the friend he's talking about? Drew Rossi and I are not friends, and I am not bringing him home with me for Christmas.

"Anyone I know?" Jim is asking and I'm backing away before I can get caught up in whatever this weird conversation is. But the heel of my shoe and the back of my long burgundy dress have other ideas. My heel snags on the dress (another good reminder about why I generally wear pants and flat heeled shoes) and pulls me down.

The next thing I know, I hit the ground hard on my butt and I feel hot liquid soak into the front of my dress and into my bra.

I close my eyes, hoping I'll simply disappear. Maybe if I pretend hard enough, when I open my eyes, this will all be a really bad dream. Except the part where I had a semi-normal conversation with Jim.

"Are you okay?" Jim's voice comes from somewhere above me shattering my daydream, and when a strong hand grabs my arm to help lift me up, I know it's not his. I'd know the feel of Jim's hands purely from his handshakes alone.

My eyes snap open and I find Drew standing in front of me, helping me up. Why on earth is *he* the one who came to my rescue? Once I'm standing, I glance down at my dress and feel my cheeks go warm. The dress might be salvageable, but I will not be saved from the fact that my boss—the man that I spend most nights dreaming about—along with the rest of the faculty and their partners can now see the snowman bra I chose to wear. Because naturally, I don't own a solid-colored bra. Normally, I love my adventurous choices, but right now I regret everything.

chapter 2

DREW

THE FIRST TIME I saw Holly Nelson, I knew she would be trouble.

Like right now, she's trouble with a capital T. Why? Because she's the only person who can help me and for some weird, instinctive reason, I was the one to help her up, even though it was obvious it was Jim she was trying to impress.

"Let's get you home." I pull my hand out of Holly's as soon as she's standing. She glances once at Jim, confirming my suspicions of her feelings for the one man I can call a friend.

But despite looking as though she might protest my suggestion, Holly stands tall and I *do not look* at the tiny snowmen that I can see through her dress and I follow her out. I glance back toward Adrienne and Felix, but Felix gives me a nod as if he knows I need this.

And it's not that I want any part of this situation. I generally stay home. I like being home, away from other adults. If I didn't need Holly's help though, I wouldn't be here at all. And then she needed my help.

"I cannot believe that just happened." Holly is laughing as we make our way into the cool, rainy night. It's been so hot recently that I should be grateful for the rain. But I rode my bike to the high school.

I'm about to tell her that she'll laugh about it someday, when it hits me that she's already laughing. How is she not embarrassed? My whole body is on edge and I'm not the one who flashed the entire faculty with a snowman covered bra.

Holly heads toward her car. "Well, this was fun."

I'm losing her. I can't lose her, not yet. I follow her closely, the light sprinkle getting heavier with each step we take.

"Hey, Nelson?"

She turns around and her blazing blue eyes punch me right in the gut. I swallow, trying to get the nerve to ask her what I need to.

"What do you want, Drew?" Holly puts a hand on her hip like she's all business, but really it makes me want to laugh because this whole thing is completely ridiculous. She's soaked to the skin with hot chocolate and I'm about to ask her an obvious question then for a huge favor.

"You go home for Christmas every year, right?" I know for a fact that Holly spends at least one week with her family every Christmas. The woman tells anyone with ears about how excited she is about it. All. The. Time. Can a person really like Christmas that much? Can someone really like their family that much?

"Yes?" Holly answers my question with a question.

"You're going home this year?"

Holly shifts her weight. The rain is coming down harder now; it's going to be a long, wet bike ride home. "Yes. I fly home on Sunday. Why?"

I swallow again. This is where it gets tricky. My mind goes back to two nights ago when I was talking on the phone with my brother, Leo. He and I don't talk much—ever really—but when he'd called me ten times in a row, I finally answered. He asked what I was doing for Christmas and said it was time to reconcile our differences and do something together. As if he is the one that gets to decide whether or not our differences can be reconciled. My jaw clenches at the memory. *Her* in a white gown, staring up at me without a hint of guilt. *He* at least had the decency to look guilty. But *both* were ready to run away and start a new life, without me.

"Why, Drew?" Holly asks again, interrupting my thoughts.

"Can I come home with you for the week?"

Holly blinks up at me in confusion. "What?"

"I can't be in California this week. I need an actual reason not to be here."

Holly gestures to the school. "Didn't Jim, I mean Mr. Sullivan, just invite you to go to Minnesota with him?"

I nod. He did, and that would be a perfect plan if I hadn't told Leo I was going home with my girlfriend. The girlfriend who doesn't exist. Leo laughed in my face, he knows my history and why I haven't dated in nearly four years. Of course, he didn't believe me. When he'd asked me what her name was, I'd been looking out my front window, watched Holly pull up to her house, and I'd blurted her name.

Leo still didn't believe me. Which is why this actually needs to happen. I can't see my brother, and while I really don't owe him anything, I don't need him showing up at my house on Christmas morning because I wasn't actually out of town.

"He did ask me," I nod again. "But I need to go home with you."

Holly tilts her head as she stares up at me, as if she's a dog and she can't figure out what I just said. "Why?"

"Just...trust me?"

Holly lets out a laugh. "Mr. Reclusive is asking me to trust him? And to bring him home to my family?"

"Just as friends."

"Duh," Holly says.

"You'll do it?" I foolishly let hope rise in my chest. She hasn't said yes, not even close. But if she did...

Holly folds her arms across her chest. "What's in it for me?"

"I'll help you out with Jim, when we get back," I answer. "I'll tell him he should ask you out." This appears to be the wrong thing to say, because even in the streetlight, I can see Holly's face drain of color. "You're into him, aren't you?"

"How do you know that?" Holly hisses at me.

Frankly, it's obvious. But I need her to say yes. "Just a hunch."

"The man who doesn't believe in love has a hunch about how I feel about Jim?" Of course, she doesn't believe me. But she's not wrong. I don't believe in love. Why she—or anyone—would want to fall in love is beyond me. Love is a ridiculous notion; it isn't real and whatever it is at the beginning of a relationship that makes people go all goo-goo eyed for each other always comes to an end.

"We're friends," I tell her again. "I can help you get him." I have no idea if this is true or not, though I do know Jim's type and though Holly might be a little young for him, it could work.

Holly stares at me like I've lost my mind. I probably have. I'll pretty much do anything to avoid Leo at this point, even if that means begging this woman to let me come home with her for Christmas. "Why don't I give you a ride home and we'll talk about it?"

"I can bike home." I'm already drenched, it really wouldn't make a difference.

"It's pouring rain." Holly rolls her eyes. "Plus, my back seat folds down, and your bike will fit just fine."

She turns and starts to walk toward her car, but I'm frozen in place. "Why?" I ask her, suddenly unsure of her motives even though it was *me* who asked her for a huge favor in the first place. But maybe she's some type of saint, I wouldn't be surprised. She always seems to be going above and beyond for any person who asks her to do anything.

"We're going to the same place, and I haven't given you an answer yet. So, let's drive and talk." Or maybe she's just practical.

I grab my bike and walk it to Holly's car, where she's already got the back seat down. I lift my bike in and head to the passenger seat, shaking my hair out before I climb inside. Holly's car smells like Christmas. There's a little Christmas tree air freshener hanging from the rearview mirror and the strong spicy scent assaults my nostrils. It's going to be a long week if she does say yes.

It's not that Holly is a bad person, she's not in fact. But even if I were the type of person who wanted more friends, I probably wouldn't be friends with her. She's too happy and cheerful to be someone I'd want to spend my time with. She acts as though life is perfect and if it's not, everything can be fixed by simply smiling and squaring your shoulders. But that's not how real life is, so I tend to avoid spending large amounts of time with people like her. People who haven't been through anything hard.

Which is probably what I should have thought about before I blurted out to Leo that Holly was my girlfriend—a detail I don't plan on ever telling her.

Holly pulls out of the parking lot and turns, heading toward our little beach bungalows. "So, you want to come home with me for Christmas?"

I clench and then unclench my jaw, wishing this wasn't my option, but the only person I can blame is myself. "Yes."

"Can I ask why?" Holly glances at me once and then turns her eyes back to the road.

"It's complicated." I swallow. "But family stuff."

Holly nods as if she knows exactly what I mean. But the fact that she's heading home to visit family for Christmas and that you can see how thrilled she is by the idea tells me that she has no clue what kind of family life—or lack thereof—I come from. And that most families probably aren't like her happy, shiny one.

"And just as friends?"

"Yup." I squirm in my seat. I guess we could call each other friends. Felix lived in my spare bedroom for about a year before he and his boyfriend decided to get married, and while he lived there, we would have occasional dinner and game nights with Holly and Adrienne. But the ones I went to were few and far between.

"Of course, just as friends. I'm not interested in you like that."

Holly snorts. "I'm pretty sure you've got a stone heart or something, because I doubt you'd be interested in anyone like that."

I ignore her jab about my heart. "But, I know that Jim could be interested in you. I can help with that."

"I can't even talk to the man without completely making a fool out of myself, so I doubt you'll be all that helpful."

"I can help you practice. I know what men like."

"No offense, but how exactly are you qualified to give relationship advice? You don't even date."

"It wouldn't really be relationship advice," I tell her honestly. "But you seem to be able to talk to me without getting nervous or making a fool out of yourself, so I could help you figure out what types of things to say so you won't be nervous."

"You don't make me nervous because I'm not attracted to you."

"So you are attracted to Jim!" I swear Holly rolls her eyes, but it's too dark for me to tell.

"Talking to him makes me too nervous," Holly says again, then gestures to her hot chocolate-soaked dress. "And makes me incredibly clumsy."

"Maybe practice will help." I know I'm begging now. I need her to say yes, but I would feel bad if I didn't give her something in return.

Holly glances at me as we come to a stop sign. "Maybe it could help." There's a fire in her eyes and I'm not sure what it means. If I were in her position, I would be going over what just happened at the party over and over again, but she seems actually okay with the idea of talking to Jim again.

"So, is that a yes?" That small flicker of hope burns a little brighter.

"It's a yes," Holly says. "But we're going to have to have some rules."

"Okay," I nod, and her phone starts to ring through her speaker. I can't tell what she's thinking as she answers the call.

chapter 3

HOLLY

Rule #2 My future boyfriend (husband) will never have a beard because they don't look good on anyone.

WHILE I WANT to keep talking to Drew about him coming home with me, Dad is calling—and I always answer my phone when he calls.

"Hey, Dad," I say as soon as I pick up.

"Hey, sweetheart." Dad's booming voice fills my car and I try not to cringe as I turn down the volume. Do I wish this conversation could be a little more private? Yes. But I guess this is what I get for having my phone connect to the Bluetooth in my car so that I can answer the phone in case anyone in my family needs me.

"Everything okay?" This is almost always my first question when Dad calls. It's not that he and I don't talk often, we do, but I still get flashbacks every time he calls me. I'm always waiting for him to tell me there's been another accident, that someone else is gone too. It's been nearly seven years now since Mom died, but I still get shaky every time Dad's name unexpectedly pops up on my screen. He knows this, and we do our best to schedule our phone calls.

But this is a random Friday night call and I'll be home in two days. Something has to have happened.

"Everything is great." I can hear the smile in his voice and I relax a little, but my fingers still grip the steering wheel in front of me and I force myself to focus on the road as I turn onto my street.

"That's good." My mind is spinning now, wondering why— if everything is okay—he felt the need to call me.

"I just wanted to let you know that Beth and I finally picked a day to get married." Dad's voice is calm and cheerful but I feel all the air rush out of my lungs.

I like Beth. She's great for Dad. But she's not Mom. And even though it's been so many years and he deserves to be happy, I don't think I'll ever be ready for him to get remarried.

"That's great," I manage to say and he doesn't seem to notice that I'm not exactly thrilled by the news. At least he's giving me ample time to mentally prepare.

"We're going to get married next Thursday! On Christmas Eve." Scratch that. There is no time to mentally prepare. And I think my body has completely forgotten that I need air to function. Thankfully, I turn into my driveway and put the car in park. "We'll get a dress for you when you get out here, but it's going to be perfect!"

"Wow," is all I can manage to say. I glance at Drew, noticing the concerned look on his face. I look away.

"I just know it's going to be incredible," Dad says before taking a deep breath. "And I know it's last minute, but you know I have to ask."

I hold back a groan at what's coming.

"I just want to see you happy. So will you have a plus one at the wedding?" All of this is happening too quickly. Dad just dropped the bomb on me that he's getting married on Mom's favorite day in the entire world—on my favorite day in the entire world—and now he's asking if I'm bringing a date? More than anyone, my dad seems bothered by the fact that I haven't found someone to share my life with yet. The questions about my dating life increased after Tally and Noah started dating, but this is the first time I feel a wave of shame crash through me. I'm too busy thinking about how I've finally become the disappointing child that I don't realize Drew is responding to my dad until it's too late.

"I'll be there, sir," Drew says and my mouth drops open in shock. I scramble to recover, to tell Drew to respectfully shut up, but Dad is faster.

"Oh!" Dad says, surprised. "And who am I speaking to?"

"Drew Rossi, sir," Drew says and I start shaking my head. What on earth is he doing?

"No. No. No," I whisper under my breath.

"Wonderful!" I can imagine Dad's face; he's surprised but thrilled. I've told him—and my entire family—way too much about my grumpy co-worker Drew and how I think he's rude, obnoxious, and that he should smile more. As well as the fact that he doesn't seem to like people in general—something I truly don't understand. But Tally told me several times that Dad has asked her more than once why I don't just date Drew, since I talk about him so much. "It's about time! Holly has told us so much about you, I wondered if the two of you would ever get together."

Yup. There it is. My dad has officially jumped to conclusions and I know we're not going to walk out of this unscathed. From the corner of my eye, I can see that Drew is looking at me, but I can't bring myself to look at him.

"We'll see you both on Sunday then!" Dad says before I can correct him. "Love you, Holly."

"Love you," I whisper and then the line goes dead.

An awkward silence fills the car. It's soon filled by the vibrations of my cell phone in the middle cup holder.

"That'll be my family," I manage to say.

Drew glances down at my phone and I can practically hear his eyes bulging. "Why are they all asking you why you didn't tell them you were dating someone or that you were planning to bring your boyfriend home?"

"I've never brought anyone home before," I say quietly.

"Anyone?" Drew asks, his tone is soft but I can't help but wonder if he's mad, or if he will be in a minute when I explain to him what all of this means.

I shake my head. "I've never had a serious boyfriend before." I've never had a boyfriend before, period. But I'm not about to tell Drew that. "And my dad, he well, he likes to think that my only flaw in life is that I've never dated anyone seriously so when you said you were coming home with me as my plus one..." I trail off. I can't even say the words out loud.

"He assumed I was your boyfriend." Drew tilts his head at me. "And you talk about me, Nelson?"

"No," I say, feeling a faint blush creep up my neck again. "I mean yes. But not in the way you're thinking. I mostly whine about how I can't believe someone as antisocial as you is the favorite art teacher at the school."

Drew smiles slightly at this.

"But my dad, he's hopefully optimistic and he recognized your name. And I'm really sorry." I finally turn to face him full on.

Tally's name flashes on the screen and I decline the call.

"What does this mean?" Drew asks, his blue eyes blinking at me.

"It means you get to come home with me," I tell him, my stomach sinking at the thought. "As my first boyfriend."

 *chapter 4*

DREW

AFTER *HER—MY brother's wife*—I always swore that I would never date another woman. I promised myself I would never fall in love again. I won't open myself up to any sort of heartbreak.

I can't *actually* be Holly's boyfriend. Even if that's what I told Leo. I don't believe in love. I don't do relationships. You can't get burned if you never let anyone get close enough to you.

"Your...what?" My mind seems to be playing catch up. "Why don't you just respond to these messages and tell them it's a misunderstanding? It's not that big of a deal, right?"

I say the words, but I already know they aren't true. In the few minutes it's been since Holly's dad hung up the phone, her notifications have been going off the hook. This is a big deal, though I can't say I understand why. Maybe it's because I've never had a family to bring a woman home to, or that when I did have a family—Leo—that he took everything away from me.

"I can't," Holly says, her voice oddly calm.

"Why not?" I glare at her as if this whole thing is her fault when I know it's mine. If I hadn't lied to Leo, I wouldn't be in this mess at all.

Holly sighs. "You know how I said just a minute ago that I've never brought a guy home to meet my family?"

"Yes?"

"Well." Holly looks up at the roof of the car and then back to me. "It's because I've never actually had a boyfriend before."

I nearly snort. "I find that hard to believe." Holly may not be the type of woman that I would date—you know, if I was into dating—because she's shorter than most women I dated in the past and the way she wears so much color should be a crime. But she is beautiful, that I can admit.

"I just haven't found the right guy." Holly tucks some of her hair behind her ear. "My sister, Tally, says it's because I'm too picky. But just because I haven't ever had a boyfriend doesn't mean I'm too picky."

I would beg to differ, but I'm silent trying to figure out how to ask my next question. "We wouldn't have to date for real, right?"

Holly lets out a huff of air and I can tell she's annoyed with me. "You really don't like me that much?"

"I..." I don't know how to respond to that, and maybe I shouldn't have phrased my question that way. But I don't do relationships and I'm not ready to explain that to her. "Tell you what. I fake date you for the week and nudge Jim in the right direction so you two can actually start dating and I don't have to be in California for Christmas. We all win."

Holly is still staring at me like she isn't sure she can trust my words.

"Please?"

"You just told me you don't want to date me for real because you don't like me but you're practically begging me to fake date you?"

I frown. "I didn't say I didn't like you."

"It was implied."

"It's not that." Does she really think I don't like her? I like her fine, just about as much as I like anyone else that I see on a semi-regular basis.

"Explain then?" Holly folds her arms across her chest and her ocean blue eyes make me look away because I feel like she's looking into my soul. I don't even look at myself that deeply in the mirror. The way she is watching me is unnerving.

I look out the window toward my own little beach bungalow. "I can't. Just... trust me?"

I expect her to roll her eyes at me or tell me no and I really will have to see my brother.

"Fine."

"Really?"

"Yes. Really. But only if you can actually get a ticket on my flight. And we have to pretend to be a couple, which I know won't be fun for either of us, but it will be easier than trying to explain that Dad was wrong, especially since he's getting married next week."

He's getting married and for some reason that makes her upset. I don't know her well enough to know why it makes her upset.

Instead of asking why she's upset about it, I grin at her. "You've got yourself a deal, Nelson."

"You've got no idea what you've just agreed to, Rossi," Holly says, then she sticks out her tongue. "Nope. Can't do it. I have to call you Drew."

"Works for me."

I'm cool and collected and confident. I'll be the best damn fake boyfriend she's ever had. And when this is all over, she can have a real boyfriend because she'll be ready. And maybe my brother will take a hint and finally stop trying to call me.

The evening air is cool as we step out of the car. "Can I come in and get that flight info?" I ask as I start to walk up the path that leads to Holly and Adrienne's place. I look over my right shoulder, expecting to see the fading glow of the sun over the ocean, but everything is dark from the rain.

"Sure." Holly unlocks her door and we step into the brightly lit and very colorful space. I have a feeling that this space has Holly's touch all over it as I take in the floral wallpaper and the bright blue velvet couch that's covered with pillows of all colors. A pair of headlights flash on the wall in front of us as Adrienne pulls into the driveway behind Holly's car.

"Are you okay!?" Adrienne asks as soon as she gets out of the car, Felix following behind her.

Holly waves her off. "Totally fine."

"Are you sure?" Adrienne asks, concern etched on her face.

"Yes. Minus my ego. Jim saw everything, as you know. So did everyone else. But I'm fine."

"But it's okay," I rush in to say, and both women swivel to face me. "I'm going to help Holly be ready to date him."

At this, Adrienne starts laughing.

"It's not funny," Holly tells her, and truly, it's not. I'm dead serious.

"I mean it kind of is. How did you pick *him* to be your relationship guru? Has he even seen your list?" Adrienne's voice softens as she focuses on Holly.

"He hasn't seen my list," Holly says in a tight voice, and I'm hit with the urge to go find this mysterious list. Does it have weird kinks on it? Or a list of things she likes about Jim? "And the story about why he's helping me is..." Holly trails off.

"What list?" I ask her, instead of explaining what exactly we'll be doing for the next week.

"It's nothing," Holly mumbles, but her face is scarlet again.

"I think I'm going to need to see this list if I'm going to help you at all." I'm grinning at her now like an idiot, but there's something like happiness springing up inside my chest and I can't seem to tamper it down. I can feel Adrienne staring at us, but I don't care.

"Why are you two acting so weird?"

Holly looks up at the ceiling, as if God or something up in the universe will help her in this moment, but as much as I'm not super thrilled with the arrangement, we're stuck. "I'll explain everything to you in a minute. First, we need to see if Drew can get a plane ticket. Actually, first I need to change my clothes. Why don't you go change too, Drew, then we can figure this out?"

Adrienne's eyebrows rise so high they disappear into her hairline. "A plane ticket?"

"A plane ticket?" Felix echoes.

"Give us like ten minutes and I'll explain everything." Holly is already walking toward her bedroom, I nod at Adrienne and Felix, and in less than five minutes I'm back to her house, my hair still wet but at least my clothes are dry. Adrienne and Felix look up at me from the couch as I walk in.

"She's in her room. Second door on the right." I feel Adrienne's stare as I walk down the hallway and knock on Holly's door. When she swings the door open, it hits me that I've never really spent any alone time with her. She's got on a Christmas sweater that could rival Santa in a competition and is braiding her hair.

"Come on in."

Her room is colorful chaos, just like the living room. But in here there's canvases all over, and an easel in one corner with a half-finished painting resting on it. I take in a sharp breath as I look at it.

The painting is of the beach, there's a woman standing, staring out at the water and even though it's not done, it's like I can feel this painting. It makes me feel like I do when I look out at the ocean, like I'm small and unimportant and yet also like my life has some magnificent purpose. It also is full of heartache.

"Incredible," I whisper, but Holly catches my word and sees me staring at the painting.

"It's not done yet." Her voice is tight.

"That doesn't matter. It's amazing. You're amazing." The words are out of my mouth before I can stop them, but I don't want to take them back. She really is an incredible artist. "Why aren't these in a gallery?"

"It's just a hobby," Holly says in a way that makes me feel like it isn't actually 'just a hobby' but it also seems to be a touchy subject. So, I let it go.

"Let's look up that flight."

Holly seems relieved by the change of conversation. I glance at the painting one last time. I can't explain the sudden urge I have to tell her that once it's finished, I'd like to buy it and hang it up in my bungalow. But I get the feeling telling her that might make her a bit uncomfortable, so instead I sit beside her on the bed as she pulls open her laptop.

"Here." She turns the screen toward me and I search on my phone. It takes a minute to load. I'm holding my breath. I let myself hope too early, and now if I can't get on this flight I'll be screwed.

"Yes," I whisper when the information fills the screen and there are still two open seats on the plane. It'll cost me an arm and a leg to book it now, but it'll be worth every penny.

"I can't believe there's a seat this close to Christmas," Holly says, her breath warm on my neck. I hadn't realized she was reading over my shoulder. We're so close we're practically touching.

"I can't believe it either," I tell her as I put in my information and complete the purchase. I let out a sigh of relief. That hurdle is officially out of the way. I won't be in California for Christmas. "I'm just grateful."

Holly lies back against her pillows. I stifle a laugh. This whole thing feels ridiculous, but I might actually have a ticket out of the state, a real reason to avoid Leo. This way, at least, he won't show up at my house wondering why I'm hiding from him, because I won't be here.

"Now I just have to lie to my family for an entire week." My stomach twists at her words.

"It'll be fine," I promise her. There's a nagging feeling in my gut about the whole lying thing, even though it's kind of all my fault. "We'll just pretend to be madly in love and then in a week, you can go get the man you're actually in love with."

Holly squints at me as if I'm a math equation she can't quite figure out. "Do you even know how to pretend to be madly in love with someone?"

I swallow. This question is too close to dangerous territory. "Yes."

"Have you ever even watched a rom-com?"

I frown at her. "What has that got to do with anything?"

Holly sighs and pushes herself off the bed. Going to the small dresser in the corner she rummages through the top drawer before pulling out a worn piece of paper. "If I show you this, you have to promise not to laugh."

My eyes widen. "Is that your famous list?"

Holly holds it close to her. "You just found out about it like five minutes ago, it can't be that famous."

"Show me."

"You can't laugh."

"I make no promises," I tell her honestly. Holly hesitates only for a moment before handing over the paper. I can tell by how the ink is smudged in some places that this is a paper she looks at often.

At the top it says *Rules for my future ~~boyfriend~~ husband.*

I look up at her. "Is this for real?"

Her cheeks go pink and she tries to grab the paper from me. "Yes."

I hold in an eye roll, because what woman in their twenties has a list like this? I remember girls in my high school making things like this, but never once they graduated. I skim her impossible list of rules. "These are all ridiculous." There is no man on earth that will check all of these boxes, not even Jim.

Holly reaches to grab the paper out of my hand, but I hold it above my head.

"And what exactly does number six mean?"

"You've never seen *While You Were Sleeping?*" Holly asks, horrified at the possibility.

"What does it mean to lean?" Maybe using a more specific question will get an answer.

Holly shakes her head, moving toward her dresser. "We have to rectify this immediately."

"Whoa, no I'm not going to watch a movie with you right now."

Holly stops moving toward the collection of DVDs. "You're right. But we will have to change that. Plus, it's the perfect time to watch it, because it's basically a Christmas romance."

"It's a romance?" I groan.

Holly rolls her eyes. "Says the man who's supposed to be my romance guru for the next week. I'm adding this to our deal: every night for the next week we have to watch one of my favorite rom-coms so that you can understand all the references on my list."

"Your list for the perfect man?"

"He doesn't have to be perfect."

"Pretty damn close." I look at the list again. "And really, what's wrong with beards?" I reach up and touch my own. Most women I know have said that they love how beards make men look.

"I just don't like them," Holly says matter-a-factly. "I feel like they would make kissing itchy and uncomfortable."

"I guess you'll find out this week."

Holly's eyes grow wide in horror. "What? No. No way. We are not kissing."

I was really only teasing, but a thought occurs to me, "Don't you think your family will think it's weird if we don't kiss? At least a little?"

"I've never had a boyfriend; they have no previous experience to rely on. For all they know I'm a complete prude."

"Are you?"

The blush on Holly's cheeks deepens. "No."

"We might have to kiss." Because now I just have to tease her about it. For some reason I like how riled up she's getting.

"No kissing unless it's absolutely necessary."

I sigh, it's not as if I actually *want* to kiss her—or anyone—but won't it be hard for her family to believe if we don't show any physical affection? This is going to be a long week. But it would be even longer if I wasn't going out of town. "Fine. No kissing unless absolutely necessary."

"Why are the two of you going to be kissing?" Adrienne asks as she walks by Holly's room.

Holly looks up at the ceiling again. "This is going to be the longest week of my life."

chapter 5

HOLLY

Rule #5: Tattoos are okay because they are an artistic expression. But no ex's names.

TALLY HAS CALLED me fifteen times since last night, and even though I'm still groggy from sleep and from everything that happened—and re-living it as I told Adrienne and Felix what was happening after Drew left—I pick up when Tally calls this morning.

"HOLLY!" She screams into the phone. "I NEED YOU TO TELL ME EVERYTHING!"

I pull the phone away from my ear and pinch the bridge of my nose. I still need to pack and get ready for my flight, even though it's not till tomorrow, but her screaming is doing very little to make me excited about doing either of those things.

"I just wish it could be a normal Christmas," I say into the phone. Tally is quiet.

When she does reply, her voice is all soft and motherly, "I know. It sucks when things change, doesn't it?"

She doesn't know the half of it. I spent most of last night

tossing and turning, not only because I am now bringing home a fake boyfriend for Christmas, but because Dad is getting married, and out of all the days he could have picked, he had to pick the middle of a week that I generally love.

"I mean, I know things have been changing since I became an adult. But sometimes I just wish that Christmas was like it used to be, when we were kids. It was like an entire week full of magic and family and traditions and I always loved it growing up, but I didn't realize how much I'd miss it as an adult."

"I feel the same," Tally says and I can tell by her still quiet voice that she's thinking about Mom too. "I miss how easy it was as a kid. Mom and Dad just made Christmas so magical, and it's always different without her. It was her favorite week of the year."

"Exactly," I say, then bring up the real reason why this year will feel weird. "And Dad's getting married—which is really awesome for him, I just don't love that he picked this week and that day to do it."

"I know," Tally says, her voice still soft. "But he's so excited. I think they've been waiting for the right time and finally realized that the right time doesn't exist, that they just have to do it. And since you'll already be in town for Christmas, I think Dad just thought it would be perfect and easy."

It makes sense, his reasoning, but it still makes my heart ache.

"I know you're sad about this, and I'm not trying to push those feelings aside, but...you've got some major tea to spill."

I roll my eyes. "No one really says that in real life, right? That's just what they say on social media?"

"How would you even know, you're on social media even less than I am." It's true. I grew up with cell phones and the internet becoming a thing but I'd like to keep my life private, thank you very much. Most social media also feels kind of like a slap in the face to art, because it's so constant and everyone can access it all of the time. But most art is slow, it takes time and feeling to create something that speaks to people. And while I don't think art on the internet always lacks that feeling, I hate the constant pressure that comes with having to put out something new all the time. Why can't we sit with what we have and slowly create new things instead of pushing out new art and content all the time?

I scrunch my face. "I don't really know. But spilling the tea sounds really weird to say. Especially since I love *drinking* tea and I do not want to spill it."

"Ha ha," Tally says but she's not laughing. "Now tell me about Drew."

Anxiety bubbles beneath my chest. It's one thing pretending in front of my entire family, but it's another thing to lie to Tally. So I opt to tell her the truth. "It's not real. I mean, he is coming home with me, something about needing to get out of California for the week, but we aren't actually dating. Dad assumed, and I thought it would just be easier to pretend than to tell Dad the truth, but now I feel bad about lying and I'm not even there yet."

"I knew it! Okay, well I didn't really know it, but I told Noah that something was up because you've been in love with that Jim guy for forever."

"Speaking of Jim, Drew is friends with him and promised to set us up once we get back from Utah."

"I thought you said that Drew didn't really have any friends."

"He doesn't. I found out last night that he's apparently friends with Jim." I tell her all about my hot chocolate mishap, cringing as I think about falling and how all of my co-workers now know I don't wear solid colored bras. I've been replaying it over and over and over in my mind since Drew left and each time, the memory feels worse. There is no way that Jim doesn't see me as anything more than a klutzy child. I am so much younger than him, and I can't seem to talk to him without being a complete fool.

"But he offered to be my fake boyfriend, even though he doesn't date. Then he suggested we should probably kiss!" My face goes warm at the thought. I still can't believe he said that thing about kissing. I couldn't ever kiss Drew.

"Well, he kind of has a point," Tally says and I gasp.

"What?!"

"Come on, Holls. Everyone knows how much of a romantic you've always been. Of course we'd expect you'd be all over your first boyfriend."

"What?" I really thought she'd be on my side. "I can't be *all* over him. I don't even like him!"

"I know. But unless you want to come clean to Dad—and everyone else—you'd better get some practice in. Or figure out how to be an actress. Gran for sure will be suspicious if you two don't hold hands and cuddle."

I groan. Why hadn't I thought this through more? We're staying with Gran. I wouldn't be surprised if she put us in the same room together—which I will not be letting her do—but I hadn't thought about the fact that people will get suspicious if I don't sort of act like I like Drew.

"I'll go talk to him later. But no kissing. I draw the line at kissing. My first kiss can't be with a man who isn't even interested in me." I lean back on my pillows. If I hadn't waited until I was twenty-eight to have my first kiss, maybe it wouldn't be such a big deal. But I did wait this long, and as ridiculous as some people think it is, I still want my first kiss to actually mean something. Which means it can't be with Drew.

"Alright, you've got me there," Tally says. "But other stuff would probably be fine. I just can't believe that he's going to be your fake boyfriend."

"I can't believe it either."

"Now you just can't fall in love with him, so that you can actually date Jim when you get home," Tally says and I can picture her, sitting on her bed, phone in one hand, twirling her hair with the other.

"Ha. Fat chance of that happening. Do you know how many rules of mine that Drew breaks? And he's so grumpy and also somehow cocky all the time. He doesn't ever date, it's like he doesn't even believe in love. There's not a chance that I'd ever fall for him."

"The lady doth protest too much," Tally says in a weird accent.

"I'm serious, Tally. He's not my type. We just have to get through this week pretending to be a couple to make Dad happy and get through the wedding, and then we can go back to being people who live next door to each other and also teach across the hall from each other at school."

"I know, Holls. I'm just giving you a hard time," Tally says, but there's a nagging feeling in my gut that maybe she has a point. Not one I agree with, but certainly one that rings true for any rom-com that has fake dating. They always hate each other, or tolerate each other, or barely know each other, and then they end up falling in love.

But that's not going to happen to me and Drew. Drew is more of a one-night stand kind of guy (from what I've seen) and I'm a settle down, get married, have a nice house with a picket fence, and a lot of kids type of woman. We are completely incompatible.

"So, that's the truth. We'll be faking it, so if I ever send you any weird looks or freeze because I don't know how to act because I've never had a boyfriend before, you can come to my rescue."

"I'll do what I can. And I'll tell you if you two need to be more convincing," Tally tells me and I groan. "I've got to go though, Noah's coming over and we're going out to breakfast and talking about our wedding details. I'm thinking sometime next summer."

"Summer weddings are great," I tell her and I close my eyes, imagining going to her wedding with Jim as my date. I bet he looks amazing in a tux and after this week, I hope I'll get to see that image for real.

"Okay. I love you, sis. See you tomorrow."

"See you tomorrow," I tell her and end the call.

I feel only slightly better that Tally knows the truth. At least I'll have someone else who knows and can help me if I'm totally awkward or weird. This is going to be the hardest thing I've ever done.

chapter 6

DREW

I'M DOING push-ups after my evening run when there's a knock on my front door. I ignore the knock—because the only people who ever knock on my door are either salesmen or religious people, neither of which are things I'm interested in—and do another push up.

Sweat drips onto the carpet as the person on the other side of the door knocks again. Sighing, I push myself up and head to the door. "I'm not interested—" I start to say as I swing the door open to find Holly standing on my porch.

The rain from yesterday is gone and the night is clear. She's wearing one of her rainbow-colored skirts and has a shirt on that says 'make art not war.'

"Oh, hi," I tell her, running a hand through my sweaty hair. "I just got back from a run."

Holly nods. "I figured. I came by earlier, but you weren't home. I saw you get back a few minutes ago. We need to talk."

My gut clenches at the last four words and I will my mind to stay present and not be thrown back in time, like it usually does when I hear or see those words. "Come on in." I open the door wider for her, focusing on the faint freckles that are scattered across Holly's nose and cheeks as she comes in.

She looks around the small living area. It's tidy and mostly black and white, a stark contrast to how this room looks in her own bungalow. Holly's eyes swivel back to me.

"I was thinking that we need a story. And probably some practice."

My mind stumbles to catch up. "A story?"

"Yeah, like how we started dating. When we started dating. My family is going to ask."

I swallow. I don't really do families. "Okay?"

Holly eyes me. "I don't know much about your family life, but growing up Christmas was a huge deal. It is a huge deal. We go all out. Activities almost every day leading up to Christmas. Lots of cousins and aunts and uncles will be around all the time. Kids will be screaming or singing Christmas songs at the top of their lungs. Someone will probably cry if we wait too long to do presents on Christmas Eve. It's an event, that's basically what I'm trying to tell you. And my family can be nosy, so they're going to want details about us."

Us. The word slams into me harder than any of the other information she just hit me with. I always swore I wouldn't be part of an *us* ever again. "Okay." It's all I can manage to say. I'll figure out how to deal with all the family stuff at some point.

"So. Did you ask me out or did I do the asking?" Holly makes her way to my couch and plops into the middle. "Huh, it's softer than it looks."

I nod. "It is. And from what you've told me about your list and unrealistic ideals for relationships," this earns me a glare, "I'm going to say that I would have had to ask you out."

"True. That would make the most sense. So you asked me out, let's say just after Thanksgiving, so it's all new but you don't have family—right?—so you're coming home to spend it with me even though it's all still new."

"Works for me." I'm still standing by the front door. I'm not really sure what to do now that we've got a plan.

"What's your favorite color?" Holly asks me.

I blink at her. "What's that got to do with anything?"

"If I was your real girlfriend, I'd need to know things about you, like your favorite color and if you listen to music and why you like running so much."

"My favorite color is maroon. I only listen to music when I have to, which isn't really often, and running clears my head," I tell her.

Holly smiles up at me. "See, was that so hard?"

Yes, actually, it was. I don't like letting people into my life. Even if it is about this superficial stuff that doesn't actually matter.

"My favorite color is forest green, but I love all colors." Holly gestures to her skirt as if to prove her point. "I don't listen to music much either, but I love having crime shows on in the background when I paint, or a rom-com. And I hate running."

I bark out a laugh. "Most people say that, but they don't actually hate running. They hate the idea of running."

Holly shakes her head. "Nope. I had a P.E. teacher in high school that made me run the mile over and over again because he thought my time was too slow. I truly hate running and you can blame Mr. Allen."

I'd like to have a word with Mr. Allen and people like him, but I keep my mouth shut.

"But just because we're dating, well fake dating, doesn't mean we have to like everything the other person does. Plus, you're a photographer, right? You look for the beauty in the world."

That's one way of looking at it I guess. I try to tell the truth with my photos, that's what first pulled me to photography when I was a teenager. It was my saving grace when I was being shuffled from one foster home to the next because no family could handle Leo for longer than a few months. Not with his unmedicated ADHD and natural ability to pretty much piss every single person off ever with the mouth he has on him. I had a film teacher who took me under his wing and helped me find myself in the world through the photos I took.

Holly looks up at me then. "Can I look at your tattoos?"

"What?"

"Your tattoos, can I look at them closer?" She stands and takes a step toward me, waiting for my response. I give her a tight nod. "Do they all mean something?"

"The first one does." I point to the sun and shooting star that is on my right forearm. "The rest were just for fun because I like them." I've got two full sleeves of tattoos at this point and I'm hoping to get more.

"I love them," Holly says in a hushed tone, as if she hadn't meant to say the words out loud. She touches the flying gold dragon I have on my left forearm with a reverence I haven't seen in someone in years. Her fingers are warm and feather-light, and send goosebumps over my sweaty body. I step out of her touch. Is my body simply reacting because I haven't had anyone touch me like that in years?

"Thanks," I say quietly.

Holly's gaze is curious when she looks up at me, like she's trying to figure me out. "I've never been brave enough to get a tattoo," Holly says at the same time I say, "you also said something about practicing?"

Holly's cheeks flush and she looks down. "I've never been in a relationship before, which means I've never cuddled with someone and even holding hands feels foreign to me. I was—I was wondering if we could practice just so I feel a little more comfortable with it. Since those are things we'll probably need to do."

"Okay," I say as if she just suggested doing something totally normal like going to grab a bite to eat and not practicing physical things with each other. "Do you mind if I take a quick shower first? I'm all gross from my run."

"Sure." Holly moves back toward the couch. "I'll find something to watch on the TV."

I take the world's fastest shower and five minutes later I'm walking back down my hallway with hair that's dripping water everywhere. I have no plan. While I know I've got more experience with relationships than Holly does, it's been years since I've done anything—even holding hands—with a woman. So, in a way I'm thankful that Holly came over to practice. I also keep having to push away my annoyed feelings of my interrupted night, since I'd planned to spend the night watching tv, albeit alone.

Holly is still on the couch when I enter the room and she's got Criminal Minds playing but she's scrolling through something on her phone.

"Hey," I say.

She drops her phone. "Hey. My cousins are wondering when they get to see a picture of you. And one of my cousins keeps asking for your last name so she can stalk you on social media."

"Your family kind of sounds intense." I sit on the couch beside her, but I'm careful not to touch her.

"They are. I love them. But I think they're feeling a tad bit overprotective about me because I've never brought home a guy before. Or dated. So, I guess this is good that it's all fake, they can't actually scare you away since it's not real to begin with." Holly looks at me and takes a shaky breath. "Can we hold hands?"

She sounds so sweet and innocent about it that I almost want to say no. I'm no good for her, but we're in this together so I scoot a tiny bit closer and hold open my hand on the couch. Holly slides her fingers through mine, and my hand completely swallows hers as we link our fingers together, but it feels comfortable.

I can tell that Holly is tense, so I run my thumb over the back of her hand. "Relax. It's just a hand."

"Right." I know she doesn't believe me. "This is totally fine." We watch the show for a few minutes before Holly looks at me again. "Can we try cuddling, maybe that will be...?" She stops before she finishes her sentence, as if she is so nervous she can't even get the words out.

"Easier?" I laugh. "You're acting like holding my hand is the worst thing in the world, and you want to cuddle?"

Holly shifts closer to me, pulling her hand away from mine. "Please don't ask me how my brain works, I don't understand it either. But I know I like hugs and cuddling seems like a long hug, so maybe it won't feel so weird. I mean, maybe it will, but I don't think it will." I notice a faint blush creeping up her cheeks as she rambles. It makes me feel a little better that she's nervous too, even if none of this is real.

"It'll definitely be weird," I say, but I lift up my arm and she tucks her small frame against me. My hand lands on her shoulder as her head falls onto my chest. This time, it's me who's stiff. Holly relaxes though, slightly, and one of her hands finds my free hand and threads our fingers together again.

Her body is warm and soft against mine and part of me wants to keep her right here forever. The thought makes me want to move and get away from Holly as quickly as I can. As if sensing my desire to run, Holly shifts even closer to me. I'm so screwed.

"So," Holly clears her throat, "I guess I should tell you a bit about my family so you have a better idea of what to expect."

Before I can even answer, Holly continues.

"There's my Dad, Joe, and his fiancé, Beth. My younger sister is Tally, she just got engaged to Noah, a guy she runs a bookstore with. We'll be staying at Gran's house, because Dad only has an apartment and no room."

"What about your mom?" I ask, Holly's mom is obviously not in the picture, if her dad is getting remarried.

"Gone," is all Holly says. She shifts like she's uncomfortable and I don't know if I'm the one making her uncomfortable or if it's the topic of conversation.

"Oh," I say.

Holly clears her throat. "I, uh, I mean. She died in an accident when I was in college."

The bluntness of her sentence hits me square in the chest. I may not know what it's like to lose someone I love in this way, but I do understand grief. "I'm sorry."

"We don't need to talk about her right now," Holly says. "How about we get back to the people you'll be meeting tomorrow?"

I nod. Point taken. "Tally and her fiancé, your dad and Beth and Gran. Got it." Five people? I can be around five people.

"Plus," Holly says and I hold in a groan, "you'll get to meet all of my aunts and uncles and most of my cousins, and their spouses or partners if they have them. And there's a few little kids too."

"That's a lot of people," I say quietly, my heart is already beating with nerves. I want to go for a run.

"They won't all be there all the time," Holly explains to me. "But I just want you to be a bit prepared, since you don't really hang out with people."

"Whatever gave you that idea?" I ask with a smile and Holly

turns to look up at me. She's so close I could count the gold specks in her eyes, which, I honestly didn't realize was a thing.

"It's just a week," Holly says and I'm not sure if she's trying to convince me or her that it's going to be fine.

"It's just a week," I repeat back to her. "I can do this for a week."

Holly's eyes narrow at me. "Are you ever going to tell me why you need to get away for the week?"

Not if I can help it, I won't. "All you need to know is that I can't be here."

"You're not like, on the run from the law or something, right? I'm willing to bring you home to my family, but I'm not willing to go to prison for you."

I'm so surprised that a laugh bursts out of me. "What? No. I'm not running from the law."

Holly blinks at me once. "Then why the secrecy?"

"I just don't like to talk about it," I tell her.

"Family stuff, though, is what you said?"

"Yup." I don't elaborate further. Instead I focus on the TV in front of me. I haven't watched enough Criminal Minds to know what's happening. Holly must sense that she's not going to get me to talk—and I really hope she doesn't take it upon herself to get me to open up about my past, I'm not that type of guy. Holly faces the TV again and we watch the rest of the episode with my arms around her and me questioning whether any of this is a good idea or not.

chapter 7

HOLLY

Rule #3: He always opens doors for me.

I REGRET every single life choice I've ever made as we stand in the security line in the John Wayne Airport. I refuse to look at Drew who's standing directly to my right. He's already asked me once if I'm okay, but I'm obviously not—which is evident from the sweat running down my face—but I'm too proud to actually admit that to anyone but myself.

When I got dressed this morning, I thought I was being smart. It's below thirty degrees in Utah, so I picked one of my favorite Christmas sweaters to wear on the plane. My brain conveniently forgot to remember that this winter has been unusually warm in Southern California and now I'm pretty sure I could wring the sweat from my clothes into a bucket. It's a disgusting visual, but it's true.

I don't think I've ever been this hot in my life.

But I can't blame it all on the sweater. I'm also *freaking out* because I'm about to bring my first "boyfriend" home to meet my family and after our practice session last night, I know I'm completely screwed.

There's no way anyone in my family is going to believe that Drew and I are into each other. Now that he's agreed to be my fake boyfriend, it's like I can't even look him in the eyes without feeling like my heart is going to explode—and it's not because I like him—it's because every time our eyes meet, I start to question everything. I keep overthinking about how close I should stand to him, whether or not I should be holding his hand now or if I should just wait until we get to Utah.

"I can hear you thinking," Drew murmurs in my ear as we move up in line. "Care to share what's got your wheels spinning so hard?"

Nope. Absolutely not. "Just feeling nervous." Gah. Dumb mouth being honest. I hate that when I'm nervous I tend to be more honest, which always seems to make things worse.

Drew gives me an easy smile as he plays with the strap on his camera bag. "Relax, Nelson. This is going to be a piece of cake. As long as you stop looking at me like you're afraid of me."

"That's the problem," I whisper to him, worried that the strangers surrounding us might actually care about what we're talking about. "I am afraid of you."

Something like hurt flashes across Drew's face.

"Not really, really," I try to explain. "More and more I'm thinking this is a truly terrible idea and I should have just told the truth but now it's way too late to do that."

"I'm your boyfriend for the week," Drew says again easily. "We can know it's fake, that there aren't real feelings here, but it can be a real relationship if that's what you need to tell yourself."

Maybe that could work. "I'll try it."

"Good, now chin up, Nelson. We've got a plane to catch."

We walk slowly to our gate—because getting through security took about thirty minutes less than I anticipated, which means we're early. Like really early. "I'm going to change," I announce to Drew and point to a bathroom. "I'm really hot."

Drew nods, because this obviously makes the most sense. If I don't get out of this sweater right now I might pass out from heat exhaustion. I'll just have to pull it out again once we get to Utah.

I hurry into the bathroom and nearly run into a tall, beautiful blonde woman who scowls at me and moves out of my way. Flushed, I hurry into an empty stall and tear my Santa sweater off my body. The stall is tiny, so getting a new shirt out of my suitcase and stuffing the sweater in makes me even more sweaty. But by the time I'm headed back out to Drew, I feel a thousand times better.

At least I won't melt now.

I stop short when I see Drew smile at the woman who nearly ran me over when I was heading into the bathroom. Something swirls in my chest and I frown at the two of them as the woman reaches out and puts her hand on Drew's bicep. I swallow, this can't be jealousy. He's not *actually* my boyfriend, so why do I feel like stomping over there and stepping between them and making him look down at me like he's looking at this woman?

It's just that I've never seen him smile, and the man is definitely smiling at this tall, blonde, beautiful woman. I should have known this was Drew's type.

Squaring my shoulders, I walk toward the two of them, stopping just short of Drew. The woman is talking, "you didn't ever call me."

Is she...pouting?

I stifle a laugh. She really didn't know Drew well if she thought he was going to call her. She glances at me for a second then her gaze goes back to Drew and I can tell she's annoyed by my presence.

"I told you, I wasn't looking for a relationship," Drew says and relief fills my body. His voice is tight and tense, he's not thrilled about talking to this woman. I mentally tell myself that I can figure out why this gives me relief later, but right now, he needs my help.

"Hey, honey," I grin up at him and for the first time since I changed, Drew looks down at me and I see a hint of relief in his eyes. "Who's this?" I look at the woman who is now staring open-mouthed at the two of us.

"I'm Melissa." She scowls at Drew. "Andrew and I dated for a brief time last year."

"It was two dates," Drew murmurs under his breath but it's so quiet that only I hear him.

"How nice." I smile up at her with more confidence than I actually feel. "I'm Holly, his girlfriend."

"I thought you didn't do relationships," Melissa snaps.

"Things change," Drew says stiffly. "Ready to go, babe?"

My stomach does a weird flip that I ignore when Drew looks down at me. "Yeah, I'm hungry. We should go get some lunch."

"Perfect." Drew holds out his hand and I slide my fingers against his. Already it feels more comfortable than last night. "Have a nice holiday," Drew tells Melissa, then pulls me in the direction of our gate and toward food.

I sneak a glance back as we walk away, Melissa is glaring at the two of us and I resist the urge to give her a wave. Instead, I turn around and lay my head on Drew's shoulder. "Good thing you've got a girlfriend. That lady gave off villain vibes."

This makes Drew snort. "Villain vibes? I didn't know that was a thing."

"It's totally a thing, and she was oozing them."

"Well, whether that's true or not, thank you. It's always

awkward running into someone who liked you a lot more than you liked them. She was really disappointed when I told her I wasn't looking for more than something casual."

"I could tell." I give his hand a squeeze. "And it was good practice for when we get to Gran's house. Not that there will be any jealous ex's that we'll have to make small talk with there. Just you and me and all of my cousins and aunts and uncles."

Drew's smile tightens again and I want to ask him why. "They're going to like you." And as I say the words, I know it's true. Drew might not be everyone's cup of tea—he's not even mine, at least not romantically—but I have a feeling my family is going to love him.

 *chapter 8*

DREW

"HOW ABOUT SOME CHINESE FOOD?" I point to the only restaurant across from our gate.

"Sure," Holly says and now that we're out of sight from Melissa, she slips her hand out of mine. I grab my camera bag strap just to give my hand something to do. "Surprise me. I'll get us some seats over there." She points to some empty seats by the big windows.

"Okay," I tell her. "Anything you absolutely don't want?"

Holly's nose scrunches as she looks at me. "I guess you need to know that I love absolutely any kind of Chinese food. You really can't go wrong."

"Good to know," I nod and head toward the restaurant. I order us dumplings, chicken low mien to share, and a beef dish that looks and smells amazing. The woman behind the counter winks at me as she hands me our food.

"Enjoy your food and fortunes," she tells me. I nod, because I'm not one for small talk, and head back to Holly.

Holly—my heart seems to stop when I see her sitting in a chair by our gate. She's one of the few people in the airport who doesn't have a phone out and I'm fairly certain she's people watching. Just the sight of her makes me smile. Her hair is piled in a bun on the top of her head. *She looks freaking gorgeous.* The thought comes so suddenly that I nearly trip over my feet. In an effort to catch myself, I run into a lady who's rushing past me.

"Sorry," I call, but the lady doesn't even seem to notice. I look back toward Holly. She hasn't noticed me yet, but I've noticed her, in ways that I am not ready for. I don't know what happened last night, but it's like she cracked something inside of me wide open and I don't know how to close it again. All I know is that I cannot let myself fall for her. She's in love with Jim, and I've seen her list—as dumb as I think it is—she's really focused on it. Plus, I'm not husband material. I'm not even boyfriend material. What I really need is a good week-long pretend fling to get all of this out of my system, then things can go back to how they were before. Me alone at home with my normal routine and no woman to distract me on my runs.

"Got the goods." I hold up the bags as I take the empty seat next to Holly. She grabs the bags from me and pulls out the food, setting the little containers on the chair next to her. Then she pulls out the fortune cookies. "Aren't you supposed to wait until after you eat to read those?"

Holly tilts her head at me. "I didn't realize you were such a rule follower, Drew."

I shift uncomfortably. "I'm not that much of a rule follower, Nelson. But I do know that if you want the fortune to come true, you have to finish your food first. And I thought you'd be into that kind of thing."

"I believe in love." Holly snorts and breaks the cookie in half, popping part of it into her mouth. "Not silly little fortunes from airport Chinese restaurants." She finishes the cookie before she smooths out the little paper that was inside. I lean over her shoulder to read it.

A romantic endeavor will bring love.

Holly laughs. "See? How would they even know that? Anyone in the airport could have gotten this, including that old couple over there who have probably been married for over fifty years. But at least it's kind of a fortune, half the time they don't make any sense." Holly reaches for the other cookie. "Should we see what yours says?"

I snatch it from her hand. "Unlike you, I like to eat my fortune cookies after I've had my food."

"Suit yourself." Holly grabs the package of dumplings and stabs one with a fork.

"I really don't get you," I say as I reach across her for a napkin and chopsticks to eat my noodles. "You have this ridiculous list for love that you believe in but you don't think that fortune cookies are real?"

Holly gives me a look that I'm learning to mean "really?"

"It just doesn't make any sense to me," I tell her.

"It doesn't have to make sense to you. My rules are important," Holly tells me by way of explanation. "And fortune cookies never come true, so why should I believe in them?"

"But you've never found love by believing in your rules, so why should you follow them?" I ask. I'm genuinely curious. She seems like a woman that men would be lining up to date, even if she does wear some quirky clothes, but she seems to push them away.

"I'm not going to talk to you about this," Holly says, and eats another dumpling. "You wouldn't understand."

"You're right, I don't," I say.

"Exactly. It's not worth me trying to explain it then."

"Does your family understand it?" I ask her and I see her bite her lip.

"Yes, they do."

I don't believe her. "Why is it so important to you?"

"Why do you hate having relationships with people?" Holly

counters. She's got me there. Why should she answer my questions if I'm not willing to answer hers.

"That's different."

"Not from what I can see." Holly turns to look at me and our shoulders brush. I hate that my entire body seems to be electrified while she's looking at me as if nothing happened, because nothing really did happen. I've seen how she acts around Jim, so why am I expecting her to suddenly clam up and get all quiet on me? "From what I can tell, you want to know this thing about me—something that most people don't understand, even when I've explained it to them—but you have something about you that I don't get. So when you tell me I'll tell you."

"Fine." I'll have to get over the fact that I'll never know why her list of rules is so important to her. Because there's no way I'm telling her why I don't believe in love or let people get too close—it would mean letting her get too close. I don't talk about what happened, with anyone, ever.

Especially not my fake girlfriend.

When Holly stands to take her garbage to the trash, I break open my fortune cookie.

A romantic endeavor will bring love.

"What the hell?" I mutter under my breath, glancing around to look over at the Chinese restaurant, but they've got a huge line and I can't see the lady who put the cookies into our bag.

I see Holly out of the corner of my eye and shove the tiny piece of paper into the back pocket of my pants.

"Get a good fortune?" Holly asks as she plops back down into her seat and I take a bite of my cookie.

"Nah, it was stupid," I tell her. "Not even an actual fortune, you know how you get those sometimes."

"I warned you."

I nod along, but I can feel the tiny slip of paper burning a hole in my back pocket. What are the chances that we both got the same fortune? The lady at the restaurant had to have known, that's why she said what she said, as some type of joke.

I adjust the strap of my camera bag to avoid touching Holly as we wait in line to board the plane. My fingers are itching to pull it out and snap a candid photo of Holly so that I might somehow capture the excited energy that seems to be oozing out of her right now. I never understood the expression "like a little kid on Christmas morning" because most of my Christmas memories aren't happy ones. But watching Holly now—as she bounces on her toes and smiles at everyone wearing something semi-Christmas related—makes me understand it a whole lot more.

"So, what are you most excited for this week?" I ask Holly as the line moves forward.

Holly bites her lip then a wide grin spreads over her face. "Probably candy houses."

I nod as if I know what this means, but I don't have a clue about what she's talking about.

"And, I really just love spending time with all of my family, it's like time passes so quickly because we're all just having a great time. It's always been that way, as if no time has passed since we last saw each other. I grew up seeing most of my cousins all the time, so it's always fun to spend time with them now that we're adults, even though so many things are differ-ent." Holly gets a twinkle of nostalgia in her eye as she's talking and I'm completely captivated. "Then of course, it's my birthday on the twenty-third, and I kind of go all out that day. We don't really do Christmas related things that day, it's all for me. Mom made sure that even though my birthday was so close to Christmas, everyone still had to celebrate my birthday as a

separate day, because everyone else gets that. Mine just happens to fall two days before Christmas. But all of it is magical and wonderful."

My mind stopped following her words the second she said her birthday was on Wednesday. "Your birthday is this week and you didn't warn me?"

Holly frowns. "Sorry, my mind has been a tiny bit busy with the whole fake boyfriend thing and my dad getting remarried."

Somehow, this doesn't feel like the whole truth. Holly just said she makes sure to have a special day for her birthday, but she hadn't mentioned it to me.

"Plus, it's on the teacher calendar, so I thought you'd already know."

"You mean the calendar they give us at the beginning of every school year with all the social events for faculty that I immediately shove into a drawer in my desk, never to be looked at again?" I ask.

Holly shoots me a glare as the attendant scans our tickets. "Of course, you wouldn't look at it, Mr. Anti-social."

"Why should I look at it?"

"So you can tell the people you work with happy birthday when they have to be at work with teens all day." Holly folds her arms across her chest.

Now it's my turn to frown. "Do other adults really like that kind of thing?"

"I do!" Holly says loudly and the woman in front of us turns around to watch us.

I hold up both my hands. "Okay, sorry. I'll look at it when we get back and never miss a birthday."

"Good." Holly looks smug now.

"But only because you think all teachers hate their jobs and need approval from other adults on their birthdays. I want to prove you wrong."

"About which part? The teachers hating their jobs or the fact that you don't think people care about their birthdays?" Holly asks and the line to get on the plane moves forward a foot.

"Both. Because I'd like you to know that I *love* my job. Teaching kids about art is one of the best things on the planet that I can think of doing. I wouldn't like to spend my time doing anything else," I say and Holly flinches as if I've struck some sort of nerve. Interesting. "And, I don't think as many adults care about their birthdays as much as you think they do."

"He's right, you know," pipes in the woman in front of us. "I haven't celebrated a birthday in nearly twenty years and I'm completely fine."

Holly's face tells me that she thinks this is the worst possible thing. "I'm going to make you like celebrating things," she whispers to me. "Because what else is the point of life if we can't celebrate things among the mundane day to day life?"

"There's a lot more to life than looking forward only to the celebrations," I tell her quietly. Holly blinks up at me in response and the line moves, this time enough to allow us on the plane and to finally take our seats.

 *chapter* 9

HOLLY

Rule #8: My future husband will have a good rela-
tionship with his parents (especially his mom) and his
family. Family has to be important to him.

"I DIDN'T REALIZE how close the mountains would be,"
Drew says as the plane lands. "And I didn't expect them to be so
huge."

I look out the window and see the majestic purple-blue
mountains that I grew up right next to. "I guess I've never
thought about it before." And it's true, even though I spent the
first twenty years of my life surrounded by the mountains, I definitely took them for granted. Something I've kicked myself
about before. I'm an artist. How is it that I lived here for so long
without seeing the beauty that was right outside my window? It
was only once I lived next to the ocean that my perspective
changed and I realized what I'd been blind to.

"I'll have to take some photos." Drew is still bending
awkwardly so he can peer out the window to see the mountains.

"It wouldn't be like any of my usual photos, but it could be cool."

"We'll have to go on a drive sometime. But really, you should see the mountains in the fall, the colors are amazing," I tell him. Drew takes his eyes off the window and looks at me.

"I'll have to come back then." His words feel heavier than they should. They seem to have more meaning than the simple sentence. He's a grown man, he can travel anywhere he wants. So why, exactly, is he looking at me like he is excited about the idea of coming back to Utah?

I glance down, realizing the awkwardness I was feeling when we first got to the airport is back in full swing. "My family is never going to believe this."

"Nelson, you have that little faith in me?" Drew looks offended, but I'm fairly certain he's just giving me a hard time.

"I have all the faith in you." And it's true, every time we've practiced, Drew has seemed completely comfortable and natural. Me on the other hand...

"You're going to do fine." Drew pats my hand affectionately. "I'll be right there the whole time. You can't mess this up, remember. You aren't trying to impress me. So just be yourself, but also pretend to be into me."

I nod. I can do this.

"Are you worried about spending so much time with so many people?" I ask him, changing the subject. I'm fairly certain that Drew is going to hate pretty much every second of this week. "You hate people."

Drew frowns. "I don't *hate* people. I just don't really like being *around* people."

"Which is what we'll be doing all week. So, I hope you'll be good at pretending to be around people, because I've already mentioned how my family knows me and my list really well and they'll know something is up if the very first guy I've ever brought home doesn't like people."

"Having to like other people is on your list? I don't remember that one." Drew says, still frowning, as our plane pulls into our gate.

"No." I frown back at him. "Having a good relationship with his own family is though. And I'd really like for him to get along with my family as well. And since you are the *him* in this situation for the next week, I hope you can handle being around all the people."

Drew nods once. "I can handle it. But I don't think I'll like it."

"You were the one who begged me to make this happen. To say yes to bringing you home with me in the first place. This is all your fault," I say.

"I know. And it's because I haven't seen my brother in nearly four years that I have to come."

Something sharp pierces my heart. "Why not?"

Drew's jaw clenches. "I don't like to talk about it."

"What about your parents?" I ask, maybe he still has a good relationship with them.

"Mom's been gone since my brother was a baby. My dad left us when I was six. I spent all of my childhood being shuffled from one foster home to another."

"Oh Drew, I'm so sorry." I didn't know.

Drew shrugs. "It's fine. I've had a long time to get over it."

But can someone really get over something like that? I want to ask him more about his brother, but it's time to get off the plane and face my family.

My dad is waiting for us just outside of the security check-point. I drop Drew's hand and run to hug him. He might be getting re-married, and I for sure have mixed feelings about that, but he's still my dad, and he's one of my favorite humans in the entire world.

"Hey, baby girl!" Dad catches me in a hug and I let out a relieved breath as I hug him tight. One thing no one tells you about losing one parent is how bittersweet it can be when you're with the one who's still here. I try to savor every moment I can with my dad, but all of it still hurts because Mom isn't here any more.

"Hey, Dad!" We hug for a few more seconds before I pull back. "It's good to see you."

"You too." Dad grins at me as he takes me in. "California seems to be treating you well."

He always says this. "Yup. Where's Beth?"

"She had her last dress appointment to make sure every-thing is ready. You're going to love it, well, that's what she said anyway, I haven't seen it yet." Dad's voice gets all soft as he talks about Beth, and the ache in my heart eases just a teeny, tiny bit. This will be good for him. It's good for him to be living his life again. At least that's what I'm going to keep reminding myself.

"I can't wait," I tell him. Then I turn toward Drew. "This is Drew."

Dad's grin grows wider as he holds out a hand. "Nice to meet you, son."

I see Drew's jaw clench as he shakes hands with my father, but he gives my dad a smile that actually looks real. I didn't think Drew was capable of that, but maybe this will actually work.

"Nice to meet you too, sir."

Dad laughs as they drop hands. "No need to be so formal, son. Joe is just fine."

Drew gives a curt nod and we head toward the baggage claim. I'm grateful that my dad didn't pull him into a hug, his normal way of greeting someone new, but my heart still starts to beat faster.

"You can do this, Holly," I whisper under my breath.

"What was that?" Drew's head whips to mine.

"There's no way you heard me," I tell him. "I was whispering to myself."

"I heard your whisper. I just didn't catch what you were saying," Drew says and I resist an eyeroll. He not only is Mr. Grumpy and Mr. Leave Me Alone but apparently, he's also Mr. I Can Hear Your Whisper in A Crowded Airport.

"Nothing important."

"Well, that's good, Nelson. Because it's show time." He grabs my hand as we follow my dad to the car.

We make it to my dad's car without any incident, where he then insists I sit in the back with Drew since we're a couple.

"Tell me all about yourself." Dad looks over his shoulder at the two of us as he pulls out of the parking spot. "I need to know what kind of man my daughter finally agreed to date."

Drew laughs—he laughs—at this. "She is a stubborn one, my Holly."

I look at him so quickly it feels like I pinch a nerve or a muscle in my neck. Drew gives me a little shrug like 'what' and keeps talking. I tune out as he starts to tell my dad about how he's a photographer just for fun but his main passion is teaching art to high school students.

He called me Holly, I've never heard him use my first name before and now I'm sitting here like a complete idiot in shock because a man—who I don't even like—said my name.

And put the word 'my' in front of it. As if I'm really his. Which, I am for the week, but that's beside the point. I'll have to add another rule about how he says my name. He can't call me his. Everyone will know I'm his, so it's not like he needs to announce that. There's absolutely no reason for him to say anything like that.

Drew's knee bumps against mine. "You still with us?"

"What? Sorry," I say and Dad smiles back at me in the rearview mirror.

"Holly's always getting lost in her own head." My face flames, even if it is the truth. It's embarrassing that I can't stay focused on a given conversation most of the time. "Sweetheart, I asked how work is going. It sounds like Drew is a great co-teacher."

"We don't teach together, just across the hall from each other," I manage to say. "But school is fine, just the usual. I'm grateful for the break."

I'm pretty sure Drew murmurs "I'm not" but before I can ask him what he means, Dad is asking him about where he grew up and if he's ever visited Utah before.

"Can't say I have. The size of the mountains caught me off guard. I don't do much traveling," Drew says and I notice that his knee is still pressed up against mine. The backseat of my dad's Civic isn't huge, but we could have our own space.

"They're stunning, that's for sure. Holly will have to take you up on a drive. It's pretty amazing how small you feel when you're surrounded by the mountains, it makes God feel pretty great."

"Yeah, sure," Drew says. I know he's not a religious person, not that I really am either, but I wonder if talk about God makes him uncomfortable at all.

"Anyway, did Holly tell you about everything we'll be doing this week..." Dad starts to go over the plan for the week, and I tune out again as I watch the familiar buildings and signs whiz by as we head to Gran's house.

DREW

WE PULL up to Holly's grandmother's house about an hour later—since her dad lives in a small one bedroom apartment, we'll be staying with Gran. It's in an older neighborhood but the house is nice looking. Even in the daylight, I can see the Christmas lights that surround the roof and the silhouette of a Christmas tree in the big window upstairs.

"You okay?" Holly whispers as her dad gets out of the car.

"Is now a good time to mention that I also don't like Christmas?" I whisper back, even though there's no way her dad can hear us as he heads to the back of the car to unload our luggage.

Holly laughs, a featherlight sound that seems to tickle my senses.

I frown at her. "That's funny to you?"

Holly is still laughing as she meets my eyes. "It looks like you really chose the wrong person to be your fake girlfriend. Did you not listen to a thing I told you about this week? About how big of a deal Christmas is to me and to my family?"

My frown turns into a grimace. "I was kind of hoping you were exaggerating and that we'd just be hanging out and watching all those rom-coms or whatever you said we were going to do."

Holly shakes her head. "No exaggerations here. But there will also be romance movies every evening to help you wind down."

The only thing that's going to help me wind down is going running every morning. But I don't get a chance to say that because the door swings open. "Well, are the two of you coming or what?" Holly's dad beams at her as she slides out of the car and then he smiles at me. I follow Holly up the front steps and through the dark wooden door that opens up to a small landing, with stairs going up and down.

The smells of cookies and something else that's probably Christmassy hits me hard. I push back all the negative thoughts forming in my head and force a smile. I can do this.

I take Holly's hand as we climb the stairs and head into a kitchen where a woman—who I assume is Tally—sits at the counter while an older woman stirs something on the stove. "Look who's here!" Joe announces as he enters the room and both women stop what they're doing and look at us.

"Holls!" Tally moves first, jumping off the stool and quickly closing the distance between her and her sister. They hug for what seems like eternity, and I realize I don't think I've ever liked anyone that much. I ignore the weird lump in my throat.

"Hi," Tally turns to me once she's finished hugging her sister. "I'm Tally, Holly's sister. She's told me so much about you, it's nice to finally meet you."

"Nice to meet you too." Surprisingly, my voice comes out normal and no one seems to notice that I'm uncomfortable. The older woman moves toward us.

"Come here, my girl," she says to Holly before wrapping her in a giant hug. What is it with this family and hugging? They seem to do it a lot more than the average family. Holly seems to melt into her, as if she's been waiting for this moment.

"Hi, Gran."

Gran releases Holly then turns to me. "Come here, my boy. You're part of this family now and we're huggers, so get over here." I'm frozen at first but then I catch Holly's eye over Gran's shoulder and I move in.

Gran's arms wrap tightly around me and I find myself hugging her back. She's soft and warm and smells like bread. The lump in my throat is getting harder to ignore, but I can't explain why it's there. I don't think I've ever had a hug like this. "You can call me Gran."

"Drew," I tell her as she releases me and I see a twinkle in her eye.

"Oh, I know."

By the time Holly leads me downstairs to show me the room I'll be staying in, I've shoved all the weird feelings I had when we first got here into a nice little box that I put in the back of my brain. Pretending to be her boyfriend, pretty sure I can do that. Confronting all the things her family makes me feel? Yeah, that's not going to happen.

"Not even going to give Gran a chance to put us together?" I waggle my eyebrows at her. I'm pretty sure Gran had started to say that the room at the end of the hallway *upstairs* would be ours, when Holly interrupted and said she'd show me the guest room *downstairs*.

Holly's cheeks turn pink, making her blush and teasing her like this is the perfect distraction from all of the things I'm really *not* feeling. "No."

"Why not, Nelson? Afraid of what might happen if we stay in the same room together?" We're talking quietly, though I'm fairly certain no one upstairs could hear us even if they tried.

"No." Holly drags out the word. "Gosh, are you always this insufferable? We're not sleeping together."

My eyebrows shoot up. "I never said anything about sleeping with each other, just that we'd share a room, like you predicted. I'm pretty sure your grandma was seconds away from suggesting that."

Holly shoves my arm. "Not like that. That is *not* what I meant. I meant sleeping, like actually sleeping, in the same bed. It will not be happening."

"Why not? Afraid I'll bite?" I joke with her.

Holly looks up at the ceiling. "What did I do to deserve this? Maybe I should let you sleep in the same bed as me and you'll see what I mean."

"What, is it really that bad?"

"I've been told that my arms and legs become part ninja when I'm asleep and no one in a close radius is safe."

I take a tiny step back from her. "Sounds painful."

Holly shrugs. "I'm only saving you from a bruised arm or shin."

For the first time, I look into the room we've stepped into. The bed, with a soft looking floral comforter, takes up most of the room.

"It's not much, but it'll be a quiet place to sleep. The bathroom is next door on the left, just in the hallway. And you've seen the kitchen."

"Can I see your room?" I give her a sly grin, and she bites her cheek like she's holding back a snide remark.

"Why would you need to know where that is?"

"Just in case I have a question in the middle of the night."

"What on earth would you have to ask me that couldn't wait until morning?" Holly looks at me like I've just suggested we commit murder and not that I may disrupt her sleep.

"I don't know, I might need to tell you goodbye before I head out on my morning run."

Her nose scrunches. "No thank you. Now do you want to go relax before everyone else gets here?"

"Everyone else?" Last time I checked, Christmas is still five days away.

Holly nods. "Caroling is tonight, remember? We go the Sunday night before Christmas every year. It's really fun."

Binge watching a cooking show over the weekend is fun. Going to an occasional basketball or baseball game with Jim—or even alone—is fun. Walking on the beach is fun. Singing to random people in the freezing cold? That does not sound like fun.

Holly touches my arm. Her fingertips send heat throughout my entire body. "It really will be great, I promise. I mean, I don't know if Christmas will ever feel as magical as it did when I was kid, but the traditions help." I feel a pang in my chest. I am not a traditions guy, unless you count going grocery shopping every Sunday morning to prepare for the week ahead as a tradition and somehow I don't think Holly would think that.

"I wouldn't know." Holly gets that look in her eyes again. The one she got earlier when we were talking about her family and I told her I don't know what it's like to have a family. "You don't need to feel upset about that. I'm fine, really."

"Ah yes." Holly snorts. "You're such a well-adjusted adult in society. You have no friends and you love to run. I'm going to show you that there's more to life than that."

"You really don't have to do that."

She shrugs. "Too bad, you're the one that's stuck with me

for a week. And I'm about as opposite as they come from you. I love people and traditions and doing fun things. By the end of the week you will too, and maybe you can get a real girlfriend."

This time, it's me who rolls my eyes. "I don't want a girlfriend. I really am perfectly happy with my life."

"I don't believe you." Holly takes a step toward me, as if to challenge me. "You run for fun."

That's her reasoning behind thinking I'm not actually happy with my life? "A lot of people run for fun."

"I'd probably die if I tried running," Holly says.

"We'll have to go sometime. When we get back to California. Running along the beach is one of the greatest things in the world," I tell her, and finally it feels like something good is building in my chest. I could talk about running forever.

Holly frowns slightly. "How about you run on the beach, and I'll paint the ocean and watch you run."

I want to tell her that she could do so much more than just paint the ocean, that the unfinished painting in her bedroom is proof of that. But instead, I simply say, "sounds like a date."

Holly's eyes flash, but she ignores my comment about the word date. "Are you going to run here?"

I nod.

"But it'll be below freezing in the morning."

I nod again. "I know, I've got some cold running gear. I'll be fine. I have to run every day."

"You sound like an addict."

"At least I'm a healthy one."

Holly laughs. "You'll be freezing when you finish."

"Then I guess you'd better show me where you'll be sleeping so I can come snuggle with you to get warm." I wink at her and Holly glances away, but I see her blush spread to her neck.

"Fine," Holly says, surprising me. "But only so I can lock the door and make you sit outside with frozen toes, Mr. Flirty."

"Mr. Flirty," I say as I follow her out of the room. "I like it."

Holly groans in exasperation and it's quickly becoming one of my favorite sounds.

HOLLY

Rule #6: He has to lean (like in While You Were Sleeping)

WE MAKE our way upstairs and I drop my bag off in my room while showing Drew where I'll be staying for the next week. It's cramped and cozy, but I love it. Gran even put in a table so that I can paint while I'm here, even though there probably won't be time. I have my travel paint set with me, just in case.

Drew leans against the doorframe, his arms crossed over his chest and he looks more relaxed than he has all day. When I move to pass him, he simply stays there, blocking the doorway.

"Let's go sit on the couch or something." I want to poke him, to make him move, but that feels weirdly intimate so I keep my hands by my side.

"We could hang out in here." I swear Drew is leaning forward, closer to me than he was a second ago. "Where there's no other people."

"W-why?" I stammer. I'm not used to this version of Drew,

the one that seems to be in his own head one second and then flirting (fake flirting?) with me the next.

Drew blinks and straightens himself and now I'm not sure if he was actually leaning toward me. Not in a way that would mean he likes me, but because I'm so much shorter than him. It makes sense that he would have to lean to talk to me so quietly.

"Because I don't like people." This time, I poke his stomach and he laughs. "Hey."

"You're ticklish?" I ask, and reach for him again, but he grabs my hand and his eyes flash a warning.

"You do not want to start a tickle fight." He says it so seriously that I want to start laughing.

"And how do you know what I want?" I shoot back.

"Trust me. I'm bigger than you. And stronger." Drew's eyes are focused on mine.

"Ew," Tally's voice rings out from the hallway. "I know you two are in the honeymoon stage of your relationship, but Gran wants you in the kitchen. Something about helping with Christmas cookies before caroling tonight."

I glance away from Drew, unsure of what just happened between us. He drops my hand and I follow him down the hallway. Tally catches my eye and she winks. I'm grateful she's in on my secret, but I'm not sure winking and comments like 'honeymoon stage' are really necessary.

We stand close—but are careful not to touch—when we enter the kitchen. Gran is already moving all around making cookie dough and frosting is whipping in her mixer. "Here, the two of you can start frosting the cookies that have already cooled. Everyone will be getting here soon, and they'll want cookies."

"What about dinner?" Drew grumbles to me under his breath.

"We'll eat something before everyone gets here," I whisper

back, sitting at one of the barstools and grabbing a cookie. Gran gives us the big bowl of frosting and we work without talking. The familiar sounds of Christmas songs fill the kitchen and every now and then Gran sings along.

I'm surprised she doesn't interrogate Drew. Bombarding him with questions about where he's from and how we met and if he's in love with me yet. But she seems focused on her task of getting all the cookies cut out and in the oven. Time to ask questions will come later, probably while we're caroling.

Once our fingers are sticky and almost all of the cookies have frosting and sprinkles, Drew and I escape downstairs with sandwiches in hand, where I show him my favorite spot in the house. The comfy couches in front of the fireplace.

There's also a wall full of shelves covered in books and pictures of all the grandkids. Any other guy would be curious, would start asking who everyone is and look for my awkward teenage photos that Gran doesn't seem to ever want to get rid of. But instead Drew plops right onto the couch next to me.

"I'm already exhausted." He leans back and closes his eyes. "I guess I really didn't think about what it would mean to come home with you, how big of a deal Christmas is to you."

"You really couldn't guess from the clothes that I wear to school all December long?" I ask with an amused smile.

"You also wear red and pink all of February and I've never seen you in July, but I bet you wear lots of red, white, and blue. I just assumed you were the type of art teacher that liked to dress up and match holidays. You have a very colorful wardrobe as it is."

It's true. I don't wear only black or shades of gray, and there's nothing sad beige-y about my house or any of my clothes. I live life in color...and in anything that could be semi-related to Christmas.

"I love Christmas," I tell him.

"I knew that." Drew's eyes are still closed.

"No. I *love* Christmas. And part of that is because of every-thing we do this week. And I know I've already talked about it with you, at least a little bit, so I'm not going to talk about it more because you get to experience it. It's magical, Drew."

"I don't believe in magic, Nelson," Drew says softly. I want to ask him what exactly happened in his life before now that has made him seemingly so jaded to the world, to Christmas.

"Well," I fold my arms across my chest even though he's not looking at me. "By the end of this week you will," I promise him again.

He scoffs. It is a hefty promise, but suddenly I want to do everything in my power to make it happen. Life is already hard enough without a little bit of holiday magic—or everyday magic in general—that I want to prove to him that maybe, just maybe, he can start seeing life a little more half full than glass half empty.

It's probably an impossible task. But Drew is an artist, and I can't imagine that someone who loves art could also be someone who can't see the magic—the beauty—that the world has to offer. He'll believe by the end of the week. I know it.

I leave Drew downstairs to relax a bit before the rest of my family gets here. Gran has also retreated to her bedroom for an afternoon nap. I find Tally sitting on the floor in front of the Christmas tree wrapping presents.

"Hey, sis." I sit down next to her and lean against the couch, closing my eyes. For a few minutes, I don't have to pretend and that feels so good.

"Hey. How are you holding up?" Tally asks me.

"Good. I think," I tell her honestly. "I mean, I'm already

exhausted from pretending, I hope it gets a little easier as he and I spend more time together."

"Can you hand me the tape?" Tally asks. I open my eyes and hand her the roll of tape. "I'm sorry you're already tired, you haven't even been bombarded by questions yet. I'm surprised Gran went easy on the two of you."

"Me too." I sigh, wondering for the millionth time whether or not this was all actually a good idea or not. "Can we talk about something else? Can I see your ring?" I've seen her engagement ring over FaceTime and in photos, but it's not the same.

Tally holds out her left hand and her ring shines in the sunlight. "This is very you," I tell her, genuinely happy for her—and grateful the green monster of jealousy that seems to come up when I think about her getting married stays away.

Tally grins. "It is. I felt bad at first, because Marsha—that's Noah's grandma—left this ring to his sister Annie, but I guess she doesn't believe in the idea of marriage or that she'll ever get married so she let us have it."

I know that Tally took Marsha's death hard. Tally worked in Marsha's bookstore and now she runs it with her fiancé Noah. "It's beautiful. And that's really sweet of his sister."

"It is. And I think you'll love her when you meet her for the wedding." Tally sighs.

The idea of weddings makes my stomach churn. "How are you feeling about Dad and Beth?" I ask her quietly, even though Dad left shortly after dropping me and Drew off to go get Beth before we go caroling tonight.

Tally's eyes soften. "It'll be weird, you know. To have Dad married to someone who isn't Mom, but they've been engaged for over a year, just waiting for the perfect time."

"And now is the perfect time?" I should hide my frustration, but I am disappointed that Dad picked this week to get married.

Tally shrugs. "I guess so. But hey, I'll be right here with you the whole time, so if you ever need to tap out, just let me know."

I don't deserve her as a sister. "Right back at you," I tell her, and I hope if the time comes for that, I can actually make good on that promise.

"I'm happy you're here," Tally bumps my shoulder with hers.

"Me too."

DREW

THE COAT that Gran finds for me to wear for caroling is far too snug, plus the look Gran gave me after I put it on made me want to take it off immediately. I don't know when her husband died, but this coat was obviously his. I glance around the family room that has slowly been filling with people.

Several of Holly's cousins have introduced themselves to me, telling me they can't wait to get to know me better, and I couldn't tell you a single one of their names. They have all seemed to go in one ear and out the other.

"When are we going to go?" I whisper to Holly. We've been 'about to leave' for at least thirty minutes already. I must not have whispered quietly enough though, because Gran glares at me.

Holly pats my arm. "Soon, I promise. We're just waiting for Dad and Beth."

If I was hot before, it's nothing compared to how I feel now. I'm wearing enough layers to be warm enough in Antarctica— which isn't exactly a great time—plus, glancing around at all of her extended family members makes me sweat even more.

I don't do families.

I never date—real or fake—someone long enough to be invited to get to know their parents or families. Was I really so blinded by getting away from my brother and his wife that I completely forgot that I'd have to meet every single person Holly is related to as her boyfriend?

This family seems far too happy for any of it to be real. I feel another bead of sweat run down my back as I wonder if they all genuinely like each other.

I'm fairly certain my shirt and sweatshirt under this coat will be soaked through with sweat if we don't leave soon. "Can't we just go and they can meet us wherever we are?" I mumble to Holly.

This earns me a glare from her. Thankfully, as she's turning away, I hear the front door open and there's more hugs and welcomes and finally, finally, we step out into the freezing cold air. The winter chill hits me with a wave of relief. Maybe I'll finally stop sweating.

"There's so many of you," I say as Holly loops her arm in mine. My body tenses at the touch and then fills with even more heat, but this time for an even different reason. Her family is watching though, so I ignore my body's weird reactions and look down at her.

"I told you, all of my extended family lives close. At least close-ish. Close enough to be here for all the festivities this week."

"And you all like each other enough for that?" My own memories of family life before Dad left us and we entered the foster system are hazy at best, but the clearest memories are of family gatherings. Gatherings where I tried to hide my brother and myself somewhere upstairs when all of the grown-ups started yelling at each other, drunk and angry. I remember that every time we left, Dad would swear left and right that we were never going back. But we'd be back the next week, because it meant one dinner that he didn't have to spend money on or prepare for us, and more money for his drugs.

"We all like each other." Holly tugs on my arm to get me walking. When we reach the house where we're going to sing first, Holly opens the binder of music she's been carrying and turns to "Silent Night." Someone in the front rings the doorbell and when the door opens a woman calls, "honey, the Nelson's are here!"

Then we sing. And by we, I mean I move my mouth to the semi-familiar words and hold back the laughter that bubbles inside my chest. I thought that because this was a yearly tradition that Holly's family would be musically inclined. But they are not.

They sound more like a group of cats that are howling than anything peaceful or magical, as Holly would probably say. I'm pretty sure there's not a single person singing on key.

But the woman at the door gets misty eyed and touches her heart and thanks us all profusely when we finish.

"What?" Holly asks as we head back to the street and start walking toward our next destination. "Why are you smiling like that?"

I can't help the laugh that bursts out of me. Several cousins, as well as Tally, all turn their heads toward me. I whisper so that the older grown-ups and Gran can't hear. "I thought...I thought you'd be at least good at singing if you do this every year."

One of Holly's cousins, Brody I think, or maybe it was Brady laughs too. "That's all part of the fun."

"Only people who've married into the family can sing," Tally says, then she lays her head on Noah's shoulder. "Well, except Noah, he's as bad at singing as the rest of us."

For some reason, I start laughing so hard at this and I can't catch my breath until we reach the next house. I barely compose myself before we start singing an off-key version of "Jingle Bells."

"Why do you do this every year?" I ask when we've finished.

"Don't ask Holly questions like that," her cousin Tyra says. "She'll say it's just because of tradition."

"Because it is tradition!" Holly says with a smile. "We do it every year."

"And Gramps loved it," Tally tells me. "So I think even though everyone in the neighborhood, including Gran, knows that we're pretty horrible, we do it to honor him."

"I see," I say, and then, house after house, I try to sing the words and block out the noise of Holly's family singing.

After the last house, as we're making our way back to Gran's house—and my fingers and toes are freezing—one of Holly's cousin's asks Holly a question that surprises me.

"Did you ever hear back from that art gallery?"

I expect Holly to laugh this off, to make a joke about it, but instead she says in a small voice, "they said that my stuff wasn't edgy enough for what they normally sell. But then a week later, I saw a piece that could have been mine hanging in the window."

"That blows," her cousin—who's name I cannot remember because there are far too many of them—says. "You'll find the right gallery."

"I hope so."

"I didn't know you wanted your art to be in a gallery." I lean down and whisper in Holly's ear. When she looks up at me, our cheeks brush before I pull back.

"That's the dream."

"That's great. You should finish that piece in your room. I'm sure any gallery would eat that up and want to feature you."

Holly frowns. "That was just an experiment, not what I usually do."

"You told the truth in that painting Holly, and it wasn't even finished yet. You captured grief and sadness and somehow hope all at once."

"It's not the type of thing I want to paint," Holly says in a tone that tells me this is the end of our discussion.

"Let me know when you get something in a gallery, I'd love to see it," I tell her instead. I'm not exactly one to talk about being brave and doing something outside the box. I ran away from California to avoid seeing my brother for crying out loud. If she doesn't want to paint like that, there's no way I'm going to force her.

By the time we make it back to Gran's house, I am somehow both sweaty and frozen all at the same time.

"Who's ready for hot chocolate?" Gran hollers as we all shuffle into the house. The landing is a mess of people, trying to get their wet shoes off so they can move up the stairs to let more people in the house.

There's a chorus of replies and Gran heads toward the kitchen.

"You doing okay?" Holly looks up at me and there's a spark that warms my entire body as she stares at me. I'm a bag of mixed emotions right now but I'm not sure what to say to her. I really need to go on a run, to clear my head and figure out what is happening with it. To shake the feeling I get every time Holly looks at me, because whatever this weird attraction is that I'm feeling toward her needs to stop. And fast.

"I'm okay." I finally settle on a half-truth. As long as I can get out and run in the morning, I can handle this and I'll be able to get rid of the attraction I feel toward her. I know I'm only feeling this way because she and I are forced to spend time together and I haven't spent any time like this—close with a woman—in years.

After hot chocolate, Holly decides that I've had enough

human interaction for the day and tells me that tonight she'll let the romance movie slide, but we'll have to make up for it another day this week. I'm just grateful to have some quiet alone time after the busy day we've had.

Until the thoughts start to hit and I can't stop thinking about Holly. When I close my eyes, I can imagine her smiling up at me tonight, as if I really was her boyfriend. It's been less than twenty-four hours and that's apparently been enough time for my body—and dare I say, my heart—to decide that I'm attracted to her. Like really attracted to her.

I always found her peppy attitude annoying, but now that I've spent the day with her, it's kind of endearing. It's not so much naive as she just looks for the good instead of letting the bad bog her down. And for some reason, that's pretty incredible and makes me want her even more.

"She's simply the first woman in years that has looked at you like you could be something more," I whisper to myself. "It's not *her* you're falling for, it's just the idea of having someone care about you."

Comforted by this line of thinking, I fall into a restless sleep.

The moment my feet hit the pavement the next morning, the tightness in my chest starts to ease. I didn't sleep well, I was tossing and turning and it took me far too long to wind down. I'm not used to spending so much time with so many people. I need this run.

It's warmer than Holly predicted, but it's still below freezing. Every time the cold air hits my lungs, I feel grateful to be alive. My breath fogs up the air in front of me as I start a slow jog to get warmed up, grateful I kept the hat Gran lent me last night to keep my ears warm. I'm not used to the frigid air, and I know I'm going to have to take it slow since I'm not running at sea level like I'm used to in California. But my lungs feel alive with each cold breath I take and the tension I've been feeling since we got to the airport yesterday slowly starts to dissipate. I was wiped out being around so many people, so I'm not surprised I slept as long as I did. It's nearly eight in the morning, and the sun is starting to lighten the sky from behind the mountains.

As I start on my second mile, along a main road, I notice someone ahead of me jogging in my direction and waving at me. When he gets closer, I recognize him from last night. One of Holly's cousin's, I think, but I can't remember his name.

"Hey!" he says once we're close enough to talk. "I'm Trevor, one of Holly's cousins."

"Right," I say, slightly out of breath. "I remember, kind of, from last night."

He laughs. "I don't expect you to remember all of us, there's quite a few family members and it is probably a bit overwhelming for you."

Understatement of the century.

"I didn't know you were a runner though. I live a few blocks from Gran and run in the mornings, I can run with you if you want." I don't want that. I like running alone. I like doing life alone. "We wouldn't even have to talk, I could show you the best routes though, since we don't live by a trail."

"That would be nice," I tell him and I can hear the tightness in my voice. I should probably care about being polite and making a good impression on Holly's family, but I also shouldn't care that much about the impression I make. Because why would a fake boyfriend actually need to care? "I don't mind the company, but I will say I'm not much of a conversationalist."

Trevor nods, then asks, "do you want to keep going or are you heading back soon? Do you know the way back?"

I nod. "I put the address in my phone." I tap my phone that's in my arm band, tracking my route. "I think I'm going to do another mile or so before I head back."

Trevor nods like this all makes perfect sense. "I've got to head home; my wife will be getting up soon to head to work and I'm on dad duty. But maybe we can run together tomorrow?"

"Sure." I should say no, but I find that I'm not actually mad about saying yes as he jogs in place. Maybe having a friend—or a running buddy—will be good for me while I'm here. It'll give me someone else to talk to besides Holly, and if I want to get rid of the weird feelings I had last night, that might be a great option.

"See you tonight, then," Trevor says with a wave and takes off running. He's too far away before I realize what he said; I'm seeing him tonight? I know Holly said that we basically have activities happening all week long, but I kind of zoned out because I was overwhelmed by the idea of being around people all week long.

I run another mile and a half before turning around and heading back to the house. As I slow my pace, I go over the plan I have in my mind. When I get back, I'll text Jim. I'll let him know that I think he and Holly would be great together and that when we all get back from the holiday break, he should ask her out. Focusing on why I'm here, and getting her ready to date Jim, will help me shake these weird feelings I've been having.

I let myself back into the house—which is just as still and quiet as it was when I left. I push away the disappointment that I don't need to be feeling. It's fine that Holly is still asleep. I'll be with her for the next six days anyway, and it's not like she's mine to want or miss. I head to the bathroom which is stocked with fresh towels. I slip my phone out of my arm band and send a quick text to Jim.

> Hey man! I was just thinking about how you and Ms. Nelson, Holly, would make a pretty great couple. The two of you seemed like you hit it off in a more personal way at the Christmas party, you should ask her out after the break.

I don't typically try to set people up. If people want something, they should go after it themselves. I'm not really about pushing other people to do something, even if I do think it would make their lives better. I also don't actually believe that they hit it off at the party, it was more like a train wreck. But I promised Holly that I would help her with this and I don't back down from my promises, which is why I don't make promises often, because then it means I have to keep them.

I go through the motions of my shower quickly and head upstairs, my hair still damp and my stomach growling. Thankfully, Holly is sitting at the counter with a bowl of cereal in front of her.

"Morning." My voice is quiet but she jumps, startled.

"I didn't hear you come up," she tells me and puts another bite of that sugary junk into her mouth.

"I showered after my run," I tell her. "How can you eat that stuff?"

Holly glances down at her bowl and then back up at me. "How can you not? You really don't enjoy happiness do you?"

"Is there any food I can make in this house? Like eggs? Vegetables, ever heard of them?" I should have brought my protein powder with me. I thought about it, but in the end it didn't fit into my already stuffed duffle bag so I have to live without it for a week. But stores exist. If there's no fresh food in the house, I can go get some things so I can eat my normal food while I'm here.

"Ha," Holly says. "There should be eggs in the fridge and probably vegetables. Gran doesn't eat like a toddler."

I open the fridge, relief filling my entire body when I see a carton of eggs, cheese, and some peppers. I can make an omelet. "But you do?"

"Sometimes," Holly tells me. "I've just never really liked cooking so I eat things that are easy to eat. Cereal is easy to eat."

"But it's basically just glorified dog food."

"Sometimes you should keep your opinions to yourself," Holly says and I grin at her.

"I'm going to make myself an omelet, would you like one?"

Holly frowns at me, like she can't quite figure me out. "Why are you being so nice to me?"

Gran enters the kitchen at that exact moment. "Darling, why wouldn't he be nice to you? He's your boyfriend. And if you're offering to make omelets, I'll take one. Extra cheese."

"You got it." I smile at Gran and then start looking in the cupboards for what I need.

"You didn't tell me he could cook," I hear Gran say to Holly.

I can imagine Holly shrugging but I don't turn away from the stove to look at her. "I didn't even tell you we were dating yet, when would I have told you that he cooks?"

"Well, you've been talking about this Drew Rossi for years. I would have imagined that him being a cook would have come up. Especially since you don't cook. Isn't something about a man cooking on that list of yours?"

"Gran," Holly mutters under her breath.

"What?" Gran asks. "It's not supposed to be a secret that you've liked Drew for years, right?"

"I didn't like him for years," Holly sighs. "I thought he was rude and annoying for years."

"And then he came and swept you off your feet and you changed your mind?" Gran guesses.

"Something like that," Holly says. Her voice is tight. I should jump in, help her somehow, but I have no idea what to say.

"He's even more handsome in person," Gran whispers this, but the kitchen isn't big and in the quiet of the morning, I can hear her perfectly. Gran raises her voice to talk to me. "You're very handsome. I'm so happy Holly found you."

"Thank you," is all I say as I crack the eggs into a bowl and begin to mix them.

"Ah, and humble too. You know, my Charles..." Gran starts telling a story about her husband, but I'm in the cooking zone and just like I generally do when someone is talking, I zone out and don't hear a thing.

DREW

"SO, tell me more about why Jim is your perfect man and why he follows all of your rules." *All of her somewhat shallow rules.* But I keep that thought to myself as Holly and I walk the aisles of Target, looking for candy to decorate 'candy houses' which is the activity tonight. I'm still not sure what it means. I never had Christmas traditions, so all of this is foreign to me.

But, after breakfast, Gran ushered us all out of the house, saying she needed some quiet time before everyone came over. Tally went to the bookstore she manages with Noah, and Holly and I were put on candy duty. Even though I would have preferred to stay home.

"What do you want to know?" Holly asks as she drops five bags of green, red, and white M&M's into the cart.

"Do we really need all of those?" I ask her, distracted.

"Yes," she says. "And what do you want to know?"

"What on the list fits Jim?" I ask because it's been bothering me since last night when one of her cousins asked her quietly—when she didn't think I was paying attention—if I really was her perfect guy. It seems like every single person knows why her dumb list is important to her except me and I get the feeling they are all judging me based on things Holly has hoped for all her life. "It might help me be a better fake boyfriend."

Holly thinks about this for a second while staring at some chocolate Santa's. She grabs two bags, puts them in the cart and looks at me.

"I can tell you one thing right now," she starts. I'm not sure I like the sound of her voice right now. She's in her bossy teacher mood and I don't like it. "You break so many of my rules. I'm sure my family thinks I'm absolutely crazy right now."

I'm sure they probably don't care that much, at least not as much as her. But I don't reply.

"But for now, one of my rules is that he's got to have blue eyes," she says, and I vaguely remember this being at the top of the well-worn piece of paper I scanned that night in her bedroom.

"That's your most important rule?" I ask, a part of me suddenly wishing my deep brown eyes were a shade of the ocean instead. Even though that would have been impossible, I may not really remember my dad or my mom for that matter, but I know from the one picture I have of them when I was a baby that they both had brown eyes. I was doomed to break this rule of Holly's from the beginning. "That's not even something that someone can control."

Holly looks at me like she can't figure out why I care about this so much, because I shouldn't care about this so much. I don't know why I care. But there's that nagging feeling that I've felt since I read that fortune cookie that keeps telling me that I should.

"I just like guys with blue eyes. You do have dark hair though, so that's a plus. Every single guy I've ever had a crush on has dark brown hair, I guess you could say that's my type." As she says this, I think of Jim and how he checks this box, and I guess in some cases looks are important.

"But you have a beard." Holly frowns at me and I touch my facial hair that I've had since I was eighteen.

"I'd look like a teenager if I shaved." This is something I don't actually know, but I assume. Growing up, people always thought I was younger than I actually was. It wasn't until I grew a beard that other adults started taking me more seriously.

"So?"

"Why don't you like beards?" I ask her.

Holly's cheeks turn the faintest shade of pink and she turns back toward the candy before she replies, "I think it would make my face itch when we kiss." Then her cheeks turn a deep red. "Not we like you and me, just me and whatever guy I'm kissing."

I hold back a smile. "I knew what you meant."

"Anyway. He has to have a good relationship with his family, especially his mom. And he needs to love watching movies."

Her list seems pretty shallow, at least to me. Does any of that stuff actually matter? I mean, maybe the family thing. But the color of his eyes? The watching movies thing? Maybe this is the real reason why Holly has never dated anyone beyond a first date, because she's so focused on this perfect guy. A guy that doesn't exist.

"Does that stuff actually matter?"

Holly glares at me. "It matters to me."

"Okay." I hold up my hands in mock surrender. "What else is on the list? I know I saw it, but there were like twenty things on there."

"Nope. You don't get to hear anymore. You mocked me and my list."

"How? By asking if what he looks like actually matters? If he likes to watch movies? Shouldn't other stuff matter more?"

Holly raises her eyebrows at me. "Oh, like what Mr. I Don't

Do Relationships Ever? How would you even know what types of things matter in a relationship?"

"Shouldn't the person you're with be your best friend? Shouldn't he be someone you can talk to and fight with and laugh with? The one you can see a future with. One you'd want by your side in sickness and in health? Shouldn't you be more worried about the deeper things like does he believe in God? Does he want a family? Does he have similar values as you? And what about how he treats you, doesn't that matter at all, or only his looks? Does he love you just the way you are, not expecting you to change for him because he knows you and only wants what's best for you? Don't those things matter?" My voice grows softer and more earnest as I talk.

When I finally glance up at Holly, it's like I see heart eyes in her eyes, but I know she's not looking at me like *that*. She just loves what I said because she's a hopeless romantic.

"Of course, those things matter." Holly matches my soft tone. "I just didn't think you'd care about those things."

Her words slam into me and I remember everything my ex said to me while we stood at the front of that small chapel, about to be married. She told me that I didn't give her my all, that I never gave her enough because I always held myself back in one way or another. That the only thing I seemed to care about were the superficial things. Then she proceeded to tell me that she'd found the guy that actually cared, and he just so happened to be my brother.

"How would you even know what I care about? You don't really know me or what I've been through." I can't keep the bitterness out of my voice now. She's hit a nerve and there's no point in hiding it.

Holly takes a small step away from me. "The way you carry yourself, and how you talk about people and things just makes me think that you don't really care about anything or anyone other than yourself."

"Just because I like to be by myself most of the time doesn't mean that I only care about myself. I care about the kids at the school. I care about photography. Do you really think I am that shallow?"

Holly shrugs. "The only women I've ever seen you 'date' or most likely just sleep with have all been tall, blonde, skinny. Picture perfect Hollywood but completely fake. Why else would I have thought any differently?"

"I don't sleep with those women." The urge to make that abundantly clear seems to take over my mind. "Sure, I bring them back to my place sometimes. I always stop it before it goes that far. I'm not that kind of guy."

Holly's gaze softens on me. "I didn't know."

"Now you do."

"Now I do. I'm sorry for making assumptions based on what I thought I knew."

My shoulders relax slightly, I hadn't even noticed how tense I was. "It's okay. You didn't know."

"Friends?" Holly looks at me with puppy dog eyes and I feel the mood shift, at least inside myself.

"You want to be friends with me, Nelson?" I ask, adding my usual somewhat cocky tone back into my voice. Hard conversation over.

"Yes." Holly doesn't blink at my sudden change in mood, the sudden switch that could actually prove her point about me not caring about anyone else, but I don't care. I'm not about to lower all of my walls, especially not in the middle of this random Target.

"Okay." I give her a smile, one that I know will make her roll her eyes as soon as she turns away from me. "We can be friends."

HOLLY

Rule #15: We have to be friends for at least 6 months before we start dating.

I'M a nervous wreck by the time people start to arrive at Gran's house later that night. Drew is talking to my cousin Trevor—something about going running together in the morning—so I pull Tally down the hall and into my room before shutting the door.

"I'm freaking out." I pace back and forth in the small space. "I can't do this. I can't lie to all of them for the next week and pretend that everything is normal. Last night, I kept waiting for someone to call us on our bluff. I just want Christmas to be normal this year."

"It's not going to be 'normal'." Tally uses finger quotes when she says the word normal. "There's no such thing. Plus, I wouldn't worry too much about what anyone else thinks. No one is paying that close attention to the two of you, except maybe Gran."

"I just want it to be the way it used to be. When we were

little and everything seemed so magical," I say, ignoring what Tally said about Gran paying attention, because that's just too much pressure.

"Who says it can't be magical now? You're always the one telling all of us that it's still magical even though we're all grown up. When did you stop believing that?"

I slump onto the bed. "I don't think I did. I just can't seem to think straight with Drew around. I can't help but wonder if everyone is going to see completely through me. It's hard to pretend to be in love with him, when we're barely even friends."

Tally scrunches up her nose. "Why do you have to be in love with him? No one is expecting you to be in love with him."

They don't? "But he's the first guy I've ever brought home."

"So?" Tally comes to sit next to me on the bed, putting her arm around me, and once again makes me feel like the youngest instead of the oldest. Sometimes I swear she acts more like Mom than I ever will. "We don't ever talk about the first guy I ever brought over for everyone to meet. So what if your first time you bring a guy home for everyone to meet is when you're nearly thirty. I don't think anyone expects you to be in love with him at this point. Sure, a few cousins have asked me about your list and if you're still worried about that, but everyone just wants to see you happy. So, if Drew makes you happy, they're going to be happy about it too."

"But it's not real."

Tally gives my shoulders a squeeze. "Why don't you go out there and pretend it's actually real? Just for tonight, lose yourself in the fantasy that Drew really is your boyfriend. Would you act differently than you have been?"

"Probably. I'd probably try to flirt more, even though I'm really awkward about flirting. And I'd probably touch him more."

Tally nods, like what I'm saying all makes sense to her even though none of it makes sense to me. "So do those things tonight. See how it goes. Maybe pretending won't be so bad if you keep telling yourself it's real."

"I don't want it to be real, not with Drew I mean."

"I know. But it needs to be real, just for this week." Tally gives me a squeeze. "You can do this. I know why you're doing this, because you didn't want to embarrass Dad or yourself by telling the truth, but now you're here and you just have to let it be real for the week."

"I guess you're right." I lean into my sister's embrace, grateful she's here. Grateful she knows my secret. "Now, should we go save our men from the Nelson clan?"

Noah, Tally's fiancé, was in the kitchen helping Gran make the icing for our candy houses when I pulled Tally into my room.

"Noah can hold his own. But Drew? He might need some saving." Tally stands and pulls me up with her. "You can do this."

I'm glad at least one of us believes that.

We leave my room and as I follow Tally down the hallway, I square my shoulders. I can do this. I can be the world's perfect girlfriend tonight. Drew is still talking to Trevor when we return to the family room. I make my way toward him and then, taking a deep breath, I wrap my arms around him and give him a weird side hug. I feel Drew tense underneath my arms for a split second, before his arm goes around my shoulder, pulling him close to me as he talks with Trevor about a race he once did.

"You two are the cutest," my cousin Kaytlin hollers across the room. There's a chorus of 'awws' and I feel my face warm under all the attention. But these people are my family, there isn't really any reason to be embarrassed, right?

"You okay?" Drew murmurs into my ear. I nod into his

chest, give him another squeeze before I step away from him. He's looking at me with an eyebrow raise.

"I'll explain later," I whisper, then I grab his hand and lead him toward two seats beside each other. "Now it's time for the competition."

"Competition?"

Tally laughs from across the table. "Holly didn't warn you about tonight at all, did she?"

"Warn me about what?" Drew glances at me as I sit down.

"It's not really a competition," I tell him, because it really isn't. Decorating graham cracker houses every December is a tradition my family has had since I was a little girl. It's one of the most nostalgic things in the world to be here right now. Plastic green and red table cloths cover the tables. The Christmas tree glows in the window beside us. All the candy you could ever imagine sits in bowls on the tables. "I'll Be Home for Christmas" plays from the stereo in the kitchen. My family surrounds me. It's one of my favorite things. I take a moment to take it all in and relive my childhood all at once.

Drew interrupts my nostalgia. "But you just said it was?"

"It's mostly for fun," I tell him. "But every year I pick one person to compete with. To see who can make the best, most festive house. Gran is the judge. She stays in the kitchen though, so she never knows which house belongs to which person. This year, my competition is you."

Drew leans in closer to me. "Are you sure you want to do that? Our relationship is so new and all, we wouldn't want to do anything to put us on the rocks already."

One of my cousins, Jordan, snorts.

I move closer to Drew, so close that our noses are practically touching. "I'm sure, because I'm going to win."

"Holly takes this competition very seriously," Tally tells

Drew. "I'd bet money that she's had a plan for what she's going to do since September."

Ha. A bet that she would lose, on a mere technicality. Because I did have my plans in September, but I made them in August. I just didn't know who would want to do the competition with me this year. But then everything with Drew happened and it just made sense to have him be my competition.

Drew's eyes are wide now. "You have plans."

I tap my temple. "All in here, baby."

Drew's mouth twitches, like he's about to laugh. But then Gran appears with our cardboard cutouts that are wrapped in foil that act as our base. Once she's passed out the cardboard, and made sure that everyone has frosting, she returns to the kitchen and turns up the Christmas music. She'll spend most of the night making more frosting so that we never run out.

I grab a package of graham crackers for myself and another for Drew. "Do I need to show you how to make a house?"

"I'm sure I'll figure it out, I am an art teacher after all. Plus, wouldn't it be cheating, Nelson, if you taught me how to build the house?"

I smile at him. "Suit yourself. May the best person win."

Drew smiles back and opens his package of graham crackers. Let the games begin.

Nearly an hour later, I'm realizing that I might have to admit defeat. And it's not for my lack of planning or trying. My house is a little two-story Christmas cottage. The aesthetic I was going for was cottage core and I completely nailed it with all the whites and muted Christmas colors I picked. But Drew's house looks like the freaking house in *Home Alone*. Like an exact replica and he didn't even pull out his phone to look at pictures.

There's no way I'll win against that, because *Home Alone* is Gran's favorite Christmas movie.

"I thought you didn't like Christmas," I whisper to Drew.

He barely glances at me before he replies. "I might not like Christmas that much, but *Home Alone* is a classic."

He's not wrong. But I still hate that he's probably going to win. Maybe that's a little bit petty of me, but I was so ready to squash him like a bug.

"Holly," Tally says, her voice one of warning, as if she can read my mind.

But before she can say anymore, my cousin Aly pipes in. "How did the two of you meet? I don't think we've heard."

This catches Dad's attention. I feel like I haven't talked to him at all since he picked us up. We hugged last night, but he and Beth left right after caroling and before the hot chocolate because Beth had to work early this morning. And I was not in a clear mental state to talk to anyone while we were caroling, I was too worried about what I was doing—or not doing—that would get us caught. Dad smiles at me, as if encouraging me to tell this great story.

"To be honest," I tell my family because every single person seems to be looking at us right now. "I don't remember the exact time I met him. I'm pretty sure I saw him once before the school year started, then again at our teacher meetings, but I don't really remember. I know, not very romantic." I try to shrug it off, but I feel disappointed. I always wanted to have a spectacular meet cute like everyone gets in a romance movie, something that would be completely unforgettable. But I honestly don't remember the first time I met Drew. He's been such a grumpy constant in my life for the past three years, that it's hard to think of a time when he wasn't around.

"I remember," Drew says, surprising me. We all swivel to look at him, including me. I expect him to be looking at his graham cracker house, like he has been all night, even when people have asked him questions about himself, but he's staring straight at me.

"Oh yeah?" My cousin Shane asks from the other side of the room.

"I'd just moved into my house. I had a roommate at the time, Felix. He and his boyfriend invited me over to his cousin's house that was next door. Something about having a welcoming party of sorts, but really it was just takeout between some friends." Drew doesn't seem to blink as he watches me, waiting for me to remember, but I don't.

I've had so many dinners with Adrienne and Felix and their friends that having Drew come over doesn't even stand out to me. Plus, right before Drew started working at the school, Jim had become the principal and I'd decided that he was the one for me, so I wasn't really paying attention to any new guys in my life.

Drew continues. "I didn't really want to go, because hanging out with people isn't really my thing, but I was starving and hadn't had time to go grocery shopping yet, so I said yes. I went over with Felix, and he introduced me to Adrienne, who I'm sure you know as Holly's roommate, and we started to eat the Thai takeout they'd ordered."

Drew reaches out then, and takes my hand in his. His hand is warm and our fingers seem to fit together perfectly. The room seems to shrink as he watches me, as if it's only us in the room and he's telling this story only to me. "I was getting ready to leave, when Holly came out of her room. Her fingers were covered in paint and she had headphones on. She ignored everyone in the room, washing off her hands in the sink before grabbing a container of food and disappearing back into her room."

"Sounds like Holly," Dad says. "When she gets in the painting zone, she completely shuts out the world."

Drew nods, as if he knows this to be true. "I mostly couldn't get over the fact that she was wearing fuzzy bright pink pajama pants and a neon green t-shirt that said something about making art, and it made me wonder if she and I would ever be friends, since I'm kind of an art nerd too."

I still don't remember that moment, but I know the shirt he's talking about. I got it while I was in college at an art festival I'd gone to. Everyone in my life thought it was completely ridiculous, even I thought it was completely ridiculous, but I also love it. "That is probably my favorite painting outfit."

Drew laughs. "Why am I not surprised?"

"It's comfortable and kind of nerdy and it really helps me get in the zone."

Drew leans forward so we're closer than we've been all night. I feel my breath catch in my throat. "What else gets you in the zone?"

One of my cousins laughs at something someone else said and I look away from Drew, blinking rapidly as if that will shake the haze in my mind. For a moment it had felt like the two of us were in our own little bubble. I can feel Tally staring at me, but I pull my hand out of Drew's and add another icing icicle onto my house to avoid looking at her or Drew. I'm not sure what just happened, but I've seen enough movies to know that I think we just had some sort of moment.

HOLLY

Rule #7: No kissing on the first date—he doesn't believe in kissing on the first date.

"WHAT IS TAKING HER SO LONG?" I bounce up and down. Tally and Noah took our graham cracker houses into the kitchen for Gran to judge almost ten minutes ago. Most of my family are still working on their houses. The younger kids are running around and playing, and I'm waiting anxiously for the results of my self-inflicted competition.

"She'll decide when she decides," Drew says easily. We're still sitting at the table we've been at all night, but now it's just the two of us.

"Easy for you to say, Gran's favorite movie is *Home Alone*."

Drew smirks. "Well, what's my prize if I win?"

"There's not really a prize, just bragging rights for next year," I tell him.

"Seriously. I did all that work and there isn't even an actual prize? How about this, if you win, I'll shave off my beard. And if I win, you have to do something for me."

I gape at him. "You wouldn't shave off your beard."

He shrugs. "I will if you win."

"And what do you want me to do?" I narrow my eyes at him but he doesn't look like he's plotting anything serious.

"I don't know yet. I guess we'll get to that point once we know who wins."

I hold out my hand and we shake. "Deal."

I slide my hand out of his, suddenly hyper aware of his every movement. His right knee is pressed against mine and I wonder how long it's been like that. How come I just noticed? He brushes a longer strand of hair out of his face and leans forward on the table. I notice his muscles under his sweater. How big do his muscles have to be for me to notice that? Or maybe it's just because I've seen him in a t-shirt before that I know what his arms look like.

I wonder if he's planning to add any more tattoos to his right arm, his left arm already has a full sleeve but he's been slowly adding tattoos to his right arm. The last one he got was a dragon that wraps around his bicep.

Not that I've been looking. At least, I thought I wasn't looking or paying much attention to the tattoos that Drew has gotten over the years. But the fact that I'm now staring at his arm and thinking about his tattoos tells me that maybe I've paid more attention than I previously thought. I squirm in my seat because Drew is *not* the man I should have been paying attention to, whether intentionally or unintentionally.

"Holly, Drew. I've made my choice," Gran calls from the kitchen.

Drew follows me into the kitchen where we stand across the island from Gran, our houses sitting between us.

Gran looks at both of us but doesn't say anything. "Well?" I ask. I probably shouldn't care about this as much as I do, but I've always had a bit of a competitive streak, plus I just agreed to do whatever Drew wants if he wins and I have a feeling that's probably a bad idea now.

"It was really tough for me this year. I can tell that both of you are so creative, which is something that Holly didn't get from this side of the family." Gran looks at Drew then and her eyes get misty like they always do whenever she's talking about Gramps. "It makes me so happy that you've found each other."

My heart clenches in my chest. Surely, she can't feel that way already. She's only known Drew for a day. We haven't even been holding hands or cuddling.

Drew looks down at me, so I look up at him and catch his eyes. "I'm happy she chose me," he says quietly.

I swallow uncomfortably. I hate lying to Gran, to my entire family. I should just come clean right now. As if reading my mind, Drew wraps an arm around my waist and pulls me against him.

Gran smiles at both of us again. "It's like you know each other's souls."

Okay. This is getting out of hand. Gran needs to reign it in. I may be the grandchild in our family who is known for being a tad bit obsessed with romance and romantic notions, but Gran has decades on me. Plus, she is a firm believer in soulmates, so I need to stop this conversation before it even starts. "Who won?"

I get a stare from Gran that tells me she's not thrilled I interrupted her day dream about me getting married and having babies with Drew, but she can't actually get attached to him.

"I love both houses, but I know I have to pick a favorite. I have to pick this one." She points to Drew's house. "I love *Home Alone* and it looks so great. I can't believe you did all of this so quickly."

Drew pumps his fist in the air. "Yes!"

I throw my head back in defeat. "I knew he was going to win as soon as I realized what he was making."

"Well, next year it will be fun to see what the two of you come up with." Gran grins at the two of us, and if Drew hadn't had his arm around my waist, I'm sure I would have fallen to the ground.

"Gran! You don't know where we'll be in a year." She has no idea that none of this is real. And now everything that Tally re-assured me of has completely gone out the window. If Gran is assuming that Drew and I will still be together next year, what is the rest of my family thinking? This was such a bad idea.

"I've got a good feeling." Gran winks at me. "Oh, and the two of you are standing under mistletoe."

I'm about to say that she's lying, but a look up confirms that she's right. When has Gran *ever* hung up mistletoe at Christmas time? Especially in the middle of the kitchen?

"We don't have to," Drew says when I look up at him. "I know you like to keep public displays of affection private."

"Pssh," Gran says, but I don't look at her, I'm still staring up at Drew, trying to figure out what's going on in his mind. "We're family. And the rules of mistletoe clearly state that if you and another person stand under it, you have to kiss."

Drew's eyes never leave mine, as he stares at me, his grip on my waist tightens slightly and I rest my hands on his chest. I expect him to lean down and kiss me, that's what I feel most guys would do, but Drew keeps staring at me.

"Well?" I ask him.

"It's up to you." His voice is soft and my eyes drop to his lips for half a second and my stomach flips. Up until this moment, I haven't thought once about kissing Drew. But suddenly, I wonder if his lips will feel as soft as they look.

I know it's a bad idea. I know it's against the rules that we established before coming here—and my rules for my future husband—but maybe Drew is right, maybe some rules are worth breaking.

My heart beats a little faster as I inch up on my toes and wrap my arms around Drew's neck.

Drew's eyes widen in surprise. "Are you sure?"

"Yes." The word is barely out of my mouth before Drew closes the gap between us.

His soft lips are gentle and warm against mine and for a moment, that's the only thing I'm aware of. How his lips feel against mine. They're gentler than I expected, and he tastes like the chocolate M&Ms he's been sneaking all night. My fingers find his hair at the top of his neck and I want to push my hands through his dark locks, but I will them to stay still. Drew pulls me closer, so our bodies are pressed against each other as he deepens the kiss. I move my lips in time with his.

I've dreamed about my first kiss thousands of times. None of my daydreams could have prepared me for this. Who knew that kissing would be so electrifying!

I'm hyper aware of every part of Drew that is touching me. The feather light touch of his fingers on my back. The way his lips move against mine makes my stomach flutter. I pull myself closer, Drew notices and lifts me slightly so my feet aren't touching the ground.

Drew slows the kiss and tenderly sets me back on the ground. I open my eyes when we pull apart, and our noses brush as he moves away from me.

I give him a shy smile as someone in my family lets out a cheer and a clap, and the noise of the house fills my ears again. I look away from Drew and fuss with the hem of my sweater.

Because if this whole thing is fake, then what in the world was that?

chapter 16

DREW

I AM ROYALLY SCREWED. This is my mantra as my feet hit the pavement and I make my way to the place Trevor and I planned to meet this morning.

"I should not have kissed her like that," I mutter to myself as I turn a corner and Trevor comes into view. I don't know what the hell I was thinking. One second I was telling her that we didn't have to kiss—we agreed that there wouldn't be any kissing —and the next second she was saying yes and had her arms around my neck and I kind of lost all sense of reality. I don't know what got into me.

I know that I'm very, very tired because I don't think I slept more than an hour last night. I spent way too much time replaying that kiss in my mind, and even more time berating myself for spending so much time thinking about the kiss.

Thinking about how her arms felt around me, what it was like to have her body so close. How good it felt to be kissed by her.

"Stop it," I say out loud, as if talking to myself will help my brain stop focusing on the best first kiss I've had in my entire life. It doesn't matter that it was great, none of this is real. Why doesn't my mind and body seem to get that?

"Hey man!" Trevor calls as I approach, and while I'm still slightly wary about running with another person, I'm grateful because simply him being here will help me get out of my own head.

"Hey," I say.

"How far did you want to go today?" Trevor asks me.

"Five miles?" I don't know how much I need, but I know I need to go at least a few miles.

"Sure," Trevor says easily. "I've got a good five mile route if you want to follow me."

I nod, and then we begin our run in silence.

The run helps clear my mind and I'm feeling good until I head into the house and find Holly sitting at the top of the stairs, holding a mug of something that's steaming. Still in her bright red Christmas pajamas. Then all of the head clearing the running did goes completely out the window. All I can think about is her lips on mine and how I want it to happen again, but she seems completely unphased.

"Morning." I nod up at her and slip out of my running shoes.

"Morning," Holly says with a yawn.

"You're up early," I note—she warned me she was a late sleeper, but I've yet to see her sleep past eight.

"Couldn't sleep." She yawns again and my heart catches on her words. Maybe she couldn't sleep because she was up all-night thinking about our kiss just like I was. "I was too cold but too lazy to get up and grab another blanket. So I was awake most of the night, but it was my own fault."

Or not thinking about me then. And even though it's a bad idea, I turn on my charm and grin up at her. "You could have always come to my bed. I would have warmed you up." Holly blushes a deep red and I hold back my smile. I don't want her to know that I really enjoy getting a reaction out of her. "What are we doing today?"

"No family plans today, and tomorrow is my birthday so we don't have to do a ton. I was thinking about visiting a local art studio that has a painting class every day."

"Sounds like fun."

Holly scrunches up her face. "You aren't just saying that, right? Because we don't have to go if you don't want to."

I put a hand to my chest in mock offense. "Do I look like the type of person who would say something is fun if I didn't mean it?"

"No. But, I know this week has been a lot for you."

"It's only Tuesday."

"Still," Holly sighs. "I know my family and our Christmas traditions are a lot. I know that I'm a lot sometimes. It's part of why I never make it past a first date. I love colorful things and I can be loud under the right circumstances and according to my sister, I'm really picky about men which apparently is a huge turn off. I'm not an 'easy' woman that every guy seems to want."

I cut her off. "Seems to me you aren't dating the right kind of guys. Any guy would be crazy not to see you for who you are and like that. And if they don't, then that's on them."

Holly stares at me for a moment and I wonder what she's thinking. I want to ask her, but I don't feel like we are there yet. Sure, we've held hands and kissed in front of her family, but I don't know how to talk to her about the real stuff, to ask her what she's thinking when she looks at me like she's looking into my soul—but I really would like to know why she's staring at me that way.

"But a painting class sounds fun. I haven't actually sat and painted in far too long, I think it would be a nice break from everything else." I give her what I hope is a reassuring smile.

She smiles back. "Sounds good. I think the class is at ten, so we can just chill until then."

"Great. I'm going to shower."

"You should." Holly's nose wrinkles again. "I didn't realize you'd get so sweaty running in the middle of winter."

I give her a half shrug because I can't tell her that I pushed myself harder than normal trying to get her face out of my head. Not that it helped, the moment I saw her everything about our kiss came rushing back.

"Well, have a good shower. I'm going to enjoy my hot chocolate."

"Then I can make us breakfast."

"I'll have my sugary cereal, thanks," Holly says and instead of replying, I just head downstairs.

When I enter the kitchen about thirty minutes later, Holly is nowhere to be seen, but Gran is sitting at the table, a newspaper laid out in front of her.

"Morning," I say politely.

"Morning, sweetheart." Gran looks up at me and smiles. Sweetheart? I don't think anyone has ever called me that in my life. And I don't...hate it. "How'd you sleep? You warm enough?"

Too warm actually, but it has nothing to do with the temperature in the house. "Fine," I tell her.

"Well, you can make yourself some breakfast and tell me a little bit more about yourself."

I hold back a grimace. Holly would want me to play nice and get to know her grandmother if we were actually dating. I just wish she were around, who knows what this woman is going to ask me.

"What do you want to know?" I ask as I grab the frying pan from the cupboard.

"Did you grow up in California?" Gran asks me.

"Yes. Born and raised." I hope she doesn't ask me about my family, I haven't even talked to Holly about my family history, I don't need to tell her grandma about it.

Gran nods like this is good news. "And you teach art at the school Holly teaches at?"

It's my turn to nod. "Yup. I love it." I don't elaborate, but Gran doesn't prob for more.

"Well, you seem like a nice young man. I'm so happy that Holly has finally found someone. She's held onto that list of hers for far too long, I'm glad she's finally put it behind her."

I want to correct Gran, tell her that actually, no, Holly hasn't put her list behind her, but I know that it looks that way. I'm far from Holly's dream man.

"You really do seem to bring out the best in her." Gran gives me a wry grin. "And that kiss, whew. Had me weak in the knees."

"Um." Is all I can manage because what the hell do I say to that?

"What are you two talking about?" Holly comes into the kitchen, her wet hair curling around her shoulders.

"Hi, love," I say to her and she freezes for a half second before coming over to me and wrapping her arms around my waist. She flicks my back.

"Love?" She whispers. I shrug and hug her back, taking in a whiff of her citrusy shampoo.

"Ah." Gran claps her hands. "I'll give the two of you some alone time."

As soon as she leaves the kitchen, Holly untangles herself from me, and I'm left feeling as though she took a part of me with her.

DREW

THE ART STUDIO is mostly empty when we get there.

"Holly!" A woman with bright pink hair gives Holly a huge hug. "You made it."

"I did say I would try," Holly tells her. "Mia, this is my boyfriend Drew. Drew, this is my good friend Mia."

"Ooo, Tally said something about you dating someone. He's so handsome." Mia takes me in and I shift uncomfortably under her gaze. "I mean, I'd paint you, but I'm more into women."

"Oh," I say in response to her clarification.

She laughs. "He's sweet."

Holly rolls her eyes at that. "Only with strangers." Mia laughs again and leads us to two easels set up with nice linen canvases.

"The two of you will be set up over here. In a few minutes I'll give a few instructions and then you'll be able to paint," Mia tells us.

"What are we painting?" I ask her, looking around for some sort of guide painting. All the painting classes I've ever attended have had an example and then the teacher goes step by step through what you're meant to paint.

Mia smiles. "Today it's a freestyle, based on your partner." And without any other explanation she walks away to welcome in another couple.

"What does that mean?" I ask Holly quietly as she eases out of her coat.

"Not sure, with Mia it could mean a lot of different things. She'll explain it though. Thanks again for coming, I'm sure now you're regretting it."

"Not yet," I tell her honestly.

"But you might?"

"I don't know. Just being honest."

"I like that about you." Holly smiles at me as she sits on the stool in front of her easel.

"Most people don't like my honesty. They think that I'm trying to be rude on purpose or that I'm cocky or think I'm better than everyone else."

Holly tries and fails to hold back a smile. "I won't lie, I kind of thought you were cocky and all high and mighty before I actually started getting to know you. You aren't like that at all. Even if that is kind of how you hold yourself for other people to see."

"I just don't really like people," I say somewhat defensively. "It's not that I think I'm better than them, I just don't really like them."

"But you like some people, right?" Holly asks me. "Like you're friends with Jim, and Adrienne and Felix."

Ignoring the way my entire body seems to tense when she says Jim's name, I nod. It's true, I do have a handful of friends, but I still prefer to be by myself. You're less likely to get hurt when you don't let anyone in.

"And me," Holly says it like it's not a question, but it feels like a question.

"And you, Nelson," I nod and before I can say anything else,

Mia claps her hand from where she's standing in the center of the room.

"Today's class is going to make you push yourself creatively and pull more from you personally than I generally ask for." I glance at Holly, but she's staring at Mia. "I want you to all dig deep. Tell your partner something that they don't know about you, tell them how it makes you feel, and then I want you to paint their emotion or them, or however you want to paint what the two of you discuss. I'll be around to check in on how it's going."

Mia claps her hands again and then the few couples in the room start talking immediately. I look at Holly again, unsure of what to do now. There's so much Holly doesn't know about me, but I'm not sure I'm ready to share.

"I want to be a painter," Holly says quietly and I'm thankful she's talking so I don't have to.

"But you already are a painter," I say, confused.

"I mean, yes. But I want to be a painter, a real one. One whose work ends up in galleries and museums across the world. I haven't told anyone this yet, but I want to quit teaching."

"What?" I'm genuinely surprised, she seems to love teaching and the kids. Plus, she's great at it, not all teachers have that gift or that spark that she has. The high schoolers love her.

Holly looks down at her feet as she talks. "I've always wanted to be a painter. I went to school to get my teaching degree so that I could have a backup plan because that's what my mom suggested I do. She knew I was good at painting, she would brag about me to all of her friends, I think she was just worried about the starving artist thing. Which I get, but now it feels like I'll be disappointing her somehow if I quit teaching."

"Even though you really want to?"

"Even though I really want to."

Something burns in my chest. "You should do it then."

"I don't know if I can," Holly tells me. "I love my job, I love the kids. Teaching has been an unexpected blessing and joy in my life, and a reliable income. But..."

"It was your backup plan," I finish for her. She nods.

"Well, I think you should go for it. I've seen your work, and it's incredible." My compliment is sincere, but Holly still ducks her head as if she's embarrassed. "You have real talent and I honestly think you could make something out of your work."

"Well, thanks," Holly says and then she's quiet a moment. "Okay, your turn."

Right. I shift uncomfortably on my stool again and glance around. The couple to our left has already started painting. I look back at Holly. "My brother married my ex-fiancé."

Whatever Holly was expecting me to say, it wasn't that. I wasn't even planning on sharing that, but it feels like it's time to come clean about why I really didn't want to be in California this Christmas.

"He...what?"

"Yeah." I let out a laugh, but even I can tell it sounds forced. "It was our wedding day, almost four years ago on New Year's Eve and she told me at the altar that she was in love with someone else. That she had been for a while, and that he made her feel all the things she had wanted from me but apparently never got. I was devastated to hear that she'd cheated, and then she told me that the man she was in love with was Leo, my little brother. He's three years younger than me, and she fell in love with him behind my back."

"That must have been terrible," Holly says quietly.

She doesn't know the half of it. The betrayal. The hurt. I'd practically raised Leo, did everything I could to keep him on a good path and in good foster homes when we weren't together. As soon as I turned eighteen I got full custody of him and we made our own way in the world, the two Rossi brothers taking on everything together. For so many years, it felt like life really could be a good thing. And then I met Janessa. We'd fallen hard and fast and were engaged within six months of meeting, planning a wedding only six months after that. I was twenty-six and thought I knew everything.

I did notice the nights she got home from work late, the way she always flipped her phone over when I came near her, and a million other tiny signs that I should have recognized for what they were, but I didn't. I think I was too caught up in it all. I was so ready to leave my past behind and start a real family that I was blinded and turned my head when the suspicion snuck in.

I just never thought my own brother would have been the one to do that to me.

I haven't seen either of them since my almost wedding day. Leo started texting again a few months back, letting me know that Janessa was pregnant and that he wanted to talk. He thought Christmas would be a great time, since we all had work off, then invited me to dinner.

He wouldn't take no for an answer.

"Yeah." My chest hurts like it used to when I spent so much of my time thinking about what had happened. It's been so long since I told anyone about it. "That's the reason I needed to get out of California. He was persistent that I come over for dinner, probably an apology dinner, but I don't want an apology."

"That seems like an awful lot to be holding onto," Holly tells me. It's a thought that has crossed my mind before, but one I always ignore. I'm not ready to let it go. "I'm sorry you have to carry that."

Holly reaches out across the small space between us and grabs my hand. She threads her fingers through mine and simply holds my hand while we sit and I let the emotions of sharing my deepest secret with her fill me up and threaten to burst out of me.

Eventually, her hand slips from mine and she grabs her paintbrush and a palette. She begins to put different colored paint on it. Reds and blues, and starts mixing to make a deep purple. Then she looks at me once before standing and angling her easel slightly away from me. "I'll show you when I'm finished, okay?"

I nod, only because I don't trust myself to speak.

 *chapter 18*

HOLLY

Rule #17: He has to appreciate art

I TAKE my time with my painting and we end up staying longer than the hour-long class, but Mia assures me she doesn't mind and that I don't need to rush. Drew paints beside me, until he finishes and walks around the gallery, never once coming to see what I'm doing—trusting me enough or maybe just ignoring his curiosity about what I'm painting.

Mostly, I do landscapes. Today's painting is more abstract. It's Drew, but it's not Drew. It's the colors I felt when he was telling me about what happened with his brother and ex-fiancé and how I see him now. There still seems to be so much anger and pain inside of him, holding him back from living completely, from trusting anyone.

So, I've painted that.

In shapes and colors, and when I look at my painting, I feel fear and anger and pain.

But also hope.

I added that on accident. The bright ocean blue is in stark contrast to all the other colors I used, but I think it works.

Not that I have any idea what I'm going to do with this painting once I've finished it. I can't imagine that Drew would want to keep it, and I could, but wouldn't that be weird? To keep a painting that's entirely based on someone I'm fake dating?

When I set down my paintbrush and palette, Drew is hovering nearby, as if he could sense I was almost finished.

"Done?" He asks me quietly and I nod slowly, looking at the swirling reds and deep blues that cover the canvas. "Can I see?"

"Show me yours?"

Drew nods and then grabs his own canvas, turning it to me. I know he said he wasn't a painter, that photography is his preferred art form, but it's stunning. It's the ocean at sunrise. He's captured the way it looks and feels so perfectly, the lighter sky on the horizon, the light, bright blue on the top. And a person—me, I would imagine—facing the shore line, ready for a new day.

"It's beautiful," I tell him.

"It's a new beginning," he says. "You, stepping into the unknown."

I swallow the lump that's formed in my throat. I don't know if I can quit teaching though because it feels too tied to Mom, and what she dreamed for me and I can't let that go, not yet, maybe not ever.

Drew sets his painting back down and I grab mine, unsure of what he'll think. I watch as he looks at it after I turn the canvas around, his eyes taking in all the colors and movement and the person that is both there and not there.

Finally, after what feels like forever, he says, "I really like that thread of light blue you put throughout. It matches the morning sky in mine."

I glance back toward his painting, and it does. We chose the same color in both of our paintings. I wonder if that means something. But instead of saying that, I simply look up at Drew. "Do you like it?"

"Do I like it?" He asks, sounding incredulous. "I want to take it home and put it above my mantle, Nelson."

Something like hope swirls in my belly. "You're not just saying that?"

He raises his eyebrows at me. "I thought we went over this already. I don't say things I don't mean."

I nod but have to look away from him. I can't seem to figure out what's going on in my head or my heart every time our eyes meet. I keep thinking about our kiss yesterday—the real reason I was awake most of the night. I keep trying to convince myself that I can't stop thinking about it because it was my first kiss, ever.

I never expected it to be like that, though. Do all kisses make you warm all over? Make your toes curl and want it to happen immediately after—even if it's with the wrong guy?

Last night, after I claimed to be too tired to show Drew one of my beloved romance movies, I couldn't fall asleep. I even tried my usual trick of daydreaming about Jim, but he kept turning into Drew and I don't know what that means. I guess I should have expected this, this is the first time I've really ever spent any time with a guy like this before and we're holding hands and I let him kiss me yesterday. Of course, he's going to be on my mind, and of course I'm going to be confused.

I just have to keep reminding myself that this isn't real, that none of it actually means anything to him and now I know why his heart is so closed off. He was hurt, and badly. I'm sure the last thing he wants is to fall in love with someone again. Not that I want him to fall in love with me.

"Are you lovelies finished?" Mia's voice breaks my spiraling train of thought and I'm glad. I don't need to be thinking about Drew any more than I already have been.

"We're finished," Drew says and then surprises me by turning his painting around to show her.

I feel more guarded with mine, it's not the type of work I usually do. But she nods approvingly at Drew's and steps around to look at my canvas. I hold my breath while she does.

"I think it's one of your best pieces. I'd put it in the gallery right now if you let me." Mia isn't one to mince her words either. While she's softer than Drew in her delivery, her words always ring true and for a moment, I can't find the words to speak.

I take in my painting again, but with fresh eyes. Before, when I showed Drew, I'd only hoped he liked it. Now, I'm looking at it with that critical eye I was taught to have in all the art classes I took in school. And I see what Mia sees, at least for a second.

Before my bravery runs out, I open my mouth to tell her that I'd love that, that she can have it, but Drew jumps in. "She'll have to do another one. I've already claimed this one."

"Ah." Mia looks between the two of us. "I see."

What does she see? I want to ask her, but my mouth is still frozen shut. I feel only a slight disappointment at the fact that this painting won't end up in a gallery, but I cling to the tiny thread of what Mia said, that this is one of my best pieces and I already have ideas for more brewing in my mind. Maybe something like this is what could get me into a gallery.

"Well, if you do any more like this Holly, call me. I want to see them." Mia smiles. "And not because you're one of my best friends, but because there's something here that I think you should explore."

"I will."

She nods. "Enjoy your holidays then. And say hello to Tally."

"I will." I stand and give her a hug.

As I start to pull away, she squeezes me tighter and leans

down so she can whisper in my ear. "Don't let that one go, you hear me?"

I nod, a stab of guilt shooting through me. I should have told her the truth.

"He's awakened something in your art, you need him." Mia releases me then and all I can do is force a smile, because what in the world does she mean by that? Sure, the painting I did really is something special, but that's because it's different than anything else I've done before, not because of who my muse was.

I've just pushed play on my laptop to watch *When Harry Met Sally* because it's after eleven and I still can't sleep, when there's a soft knock on my door. I pause the movie. "Come in," I call softly so I don't wake Gran whose room is across the hall from this one.

I know it's not Gran or Tally on the other side of that door because both of them would have barged right in without knocking.

The door opens slowly and I see Drew standing in his deep blue pajama bottoms and plain white t-shirt.

"Can't sleep?" I whisper and he shakes his head. "Me either. Come on in, I was just about to watch *When Harry Met Sally*. We can finally watch one of the romance movies I've been wanting to show you."

"I've never seen it," Drew says quietly as he slips into my room, softly shutting the door behind him. He stands there for a moment and I pat the bed beside me.

"I don't bite," I tell him, but he's been acting weird all day. Or maybe he's been acting normal. It was mostly just us in the house today. Tally went to the bookstore and Gran had a lunch that took nearly five hours with one of her friends. There hasn't been any pretending happening. I watched a Christmas movie alone while Drew hid out in his room claiming he needed a nap, but really, I think he was avoiding me.

He cautiously makes his way to the bed and then climbs on next to me.

"And I'm going to ignore the fact that you've never seen this classic," I tell Drew as he leans back on the pillows next to me. I can feel the warmth radiating off his body but he doesn't touch me. Every nerve on my body is standing on end for reasons I don't understand.

"Is it really a classic though?" He whispers, jolting me back into the present and away from my body's strange reactions to Drew.

"Gran won't wake up; she sleeps like the dead," I tell him in a slightly quieter than normal voice. "And yes. *When Harry Met Sally* is a classic rom-com for sure. But I'm not surprised you've never seen it. Now is your chance."

"I guess so," Drew says, not even bothering to comment on anything else. I swallow a rush of slight annoyance; couldn't he at least pretend to care? Ignoring him, I lean forward and push play on my laptop.

 *chapter 19*

DREW

BY THE TIME the movie ends, my body is exhausted and it's well after midnight. I hope I'll still be able to get up for a run in the morning, because heaven knows I need to go on one.

"Happy birthday," I tell Holly as she closes her laptop, plunging us into darkness. She reaches beside her to turn the lamp on.

"Thanks." She smiles at me and then yawns. "What did you think?"

"It was fine," I tell her. Romantic comedies haven't ever really been my thing.

"Fine!?" She asks as if she can't believe I didn't love it.

"Yes."

Holly leans back on the pillows and the bed shifts. "Well, do you agree with Harry?"

I bite my lip. "Harry does have a point. Men and women really can't be friends, one of them always ends up being attracted to the other person."

"I don't know if that's true though," Holly says. "I've been friends with plenty of men and we've always just been friends. And we're friends, aren't we?"

I take in a sharp breath, remembering her lips on mine and the unworthy intentions I'd had in coming up here to her room originally. "Yes, Nelson. We're friends."

Holly's eyes are closed when I look at her though, so she isn't watching my reaction and she takes my response for the words they are and not anything else. Because the truth is, even though I don't do relationships and I don't foresee anything happening with Holly beyond this week, I am attracted to her and I'd really like to kiss her again.

I had every intention of kissing her again tonight, but then she asked if I wanted to watch that movie with her, and she just seemed so young and wholesome. She doesn't need someone like me, she doesn't need a fling—even if most of it happens under the pretense of us being in a fake relationship—and I certainly don't need it. I just need to keep reminding myself of that.

"I should go, so we can get some sleep," I say quietly.

"Hmm?" Holly asks, she's already halfway asleep.

Then, ignoring the battle I've been having with my mind, I lean forward and kiss her forehead. It's a whisper of a kiss really, my lips barely touch her and then I'm pulling away.

She doesn't even open her eyes.

"Get some sleep, birthday girl." I slip out of her room without another word.

My muscles are screaming as I try to take in a deep breath and pick up my speed. I have to get Holly out of my head, but that's going to be kind of hard today because today is her birthday. And thanks to Tally, we have a very fun and possibly romantic day planned. Holly has no idea what's about to happen. Tally filled me in last night when she got home from work of all the activities she planned for the four of us to do to celebrate Holly's birthday.

When I get back to Gran's house, I take a quick shower and then head upstairs. Holly is still asleep, which makes sense since we were up late last night. Her question about us being friends and my answer that we are—even though I don't think we could actually ever be friends—has been on repeat all morning. This week we have whatever the hell this is, and after that, we go back to nodding politely in the hallway and seeing each other occasionally after work, and then I get to watch her fall in love with Jim.

I'm making my breakfast when Gran comes into the kitchen to make her morning toast, and then she heads out to sit on the couch and read the morning paper, just like yesterday.

"Did you sleep well?" Gran asks and I catch a twinkle in her eye that tells me she knows I spent some time in Holly's room last night.

"Mhm," I say, I'm not really in the mood to think about last night any more than I already have.

I'm saved by saying anything more when Tally comes in, looking groggy and grumpy.

"Morning," I say, grateful for a distraction.

"Hmfph," Tally says in return, and I remember that Holly told me Tally is not a morning person.

"Why are you up so early?" I ask.

"Well I have to go to the bookstore real quick before we head out today, so I'm awake and she's not even awake and I kind of want to kill her," Tally says into the fridge and then she looks at me. "But it is her birthday so I guess I can forgive her. Why are you awake? It's not even seven in the morning."

I smile into my eggs, before I remember that Leo and I might have had a relationship like that once, but now it's just best if we don't speak. "I always wake up early. I like to run."

Tally gives me the same expression that Holly did when I told her I was a runner—like she can't believe that someone would possibly ever want to run just for the fun of it.

"Are you ready for today?" Tally asks.

No. No I am not. "Yup," I tell her and she eyes me suspiciously. "The plan you made is great, I think. I hope she likes it." Tally assured me that everything we'll be doing are things that Holly will love, but I don't know Holly well enough to know for sure. There are a few activities today that I'm a little iffy about, but I'm going to try to trust Tally and hope it goes well.

Gran comes back into the kitchen. "I'm making a cake for tonight, so you'll be back in time for that, right?"

I nod. That is one part of the plan I really can't mess up. We're having cake back at the house at five sharp, because we all have to be at the rehearsal dinner for the wedding at seven. "And Holly will be fine doing cake before the dinner?"

"Yes," Tally answers. "I mean, she hasn't really said much about the wedding. Gran gave her the dress for the reception but I don't know if she's even tried it on yet. But she'll be okay to eat cake before dinner."

"We'll have her try it on today," Gran says and then looks at me. "But the two of you have a good day. Treat that girl right."

"I will," I tell her and I feel Tally's eyes on me and I have a feeling she can see right through me and all my feelings that I'm trying so hard—and failing—to shove down.

We all hear Holly's door open from the end of the hallway. "Shower our girl with lots of love today."

I nod, but my stomach clenches at the word love. Holly doesn't come into the kitchen but instead disappears into the bathroom before any of us can see her.

"Well, I did want to say happy birthday to her in person," Tally grumbles. "But I also told Noah I'd be done with the shop by eight so we can come back over here, which means I need to get ready."

I'm not in any particular rush. We do have quite a few things on our list today, but if we don't get to something, it won't be the end of the world.

I wait awkwardly in the kitchen for Holly to come out of the bathroom before realizing that standing just outside the bathroom door is probably a little weird for a boyfriend—even a real one—to do. Gran's disappeared into her own bedroom again, so when I walk into the living room, I'm alone.

The Christmas tree takes up most of the window space, the lights already on to start the morning off. It's comfortable and pretty, and I think I'm starting to see why Holly loves Christmas with her family so much.

When Holly comes out of the bathroom and makes her way toward the living room, I notice she doesn't have any of the usual color in her cheeks. "Are you okay?"

Holly shakes her head miserably as she flops onto the couch next to me. Her skin is like a furnace. I touch her head with the back of my hand. "I'd say you have a fever."

"Mhm," She groans. "And puking."

"And you're puking? We have to stay home today," I tell her as she's already starting to shake her head in protest.

"We have to go. It's my birthday." She barely gets the words out.

"Nope. We're staying home today. We've got to get you well for your dad's wedding." She scowls at this. "Just because you don't like it, doesn't mean you can say anything. He seems genuinely happy, he deserves to get married."

"Mad about staying in," Holly pouts. "Not Dad."

"Okay," I say but I don't actually believe her. She's barely spoken to her dad since we've been here, and I was there when he called and told her the news, and she was less than thrilled that he's getting remarried this week.

"We can go." She tries to push herself up.

"Nope," I say, pulling her against me instead. "I'll find out where Gran keeps her crackers and if she has any juice. We'll spend the day watching Christmas movies or more of those rom-coms you love."

"But—"

"No buts." I run a hand through her hair, and her warm body scalds mine. "And we need to get that fever of yours down. Maybe medicine and a cool towel?"

I feel her nod against my chest.

"Good."

DREW

HOLLY MUST JUST HAVE some twenty-four hour or less than twenty-four-hour bug, because around three in the afternoon, she starts to perk up.

We've been hanging out in her bedroom all day. She's mostly been sleeping—and shivering—and I've been doing my best to keep her comfortable. Switching the cool rag on her forehead, rubbing her back when she was in a fitful state of sleep, and I grabbed the huge mixing bowl that doubled as her puke bowl when she couldn't make it to the bathroom.

Twice.

I'm not someone who does well with barf, but I hate seeing her like this. I would do just about anything to give her some relief.

"Do you think we still have time to do some of the things you planned before the rehearsal dinner?" Holly's voice is a little horse and scratchy.

"Oh no," I tell her, we probably do have the time, but she's not going out after being sick all day. "We're not going anywhere today. You're off the hook for the rehearsal dinner tonight. Your dad wants you well rested for tomorrow. And we'll be able to do at least one or two of the things Tally planned before the wedding tomorrow. As long as you're feeling better."

Holly frowns at me.

"Don't give me that look, Ms. Pukey."

"But it's my birthday," she whines like she just turned five instead of thirty or however old she's turning today; I don't actually have any idea. My guess is thirty or around that. I probably should have asked.

"And you've been sick all day. Your fever barely broke. You haven't been able to keep anything down yet. Your body needs rest." Holly's frown deepens and I get the feeling that if I wasn't the one telling her to rest, she'd be up and out of this bed already. Telling everyone that she was good to go and the birthday festivities could continue.

"Can I at least go brush my teeth?" She finally grumbles.

"Of course."

Holly gets out of the bed slowly, and I don't miss the fact that she pauses at the door frame to catch her breath. While she's brushing her teeth, I double check the cracker bowl—which she hasn't even touched—and grab a cold bottle of Gatorade from the fridge. Now will be the real moment of truth, if she can actually keep anything down.

I'm exhausted and I'm not even the one who's sick today. I hate getting sick, though. I hate it pretty much more than anything. As I make my way back to Holly's room, it hits me that maybe it's not being sick that I actually hate, but the fact that when I'm sick, I still have to be the one to take care of myself. I'm the one who has to make sure I've got the crackers and juice and soup. There hasn't been anyone to look out for me in a long time, and as I enter Holly's room, ready to give her anything she needs, I realize that what I really hate about being sick is the fact that there's no one around to take care of me.

Holly is already back under the covers and I make my way

back to my spot on the bed. I hold out the bowl of crackers, and she takes one cracker out and nibbles on it.

"Hopefully you can keep it down," I say gently as I reach for her laptop. "Want to watch something?"

Holly ignores my comment and question. "Aren't you worried that you'll catch whatever this is?"

The thought occurred to me about three hours ago, when she was curled up against me and having what I assume was a fever dream, she was restless and crying in her sleep. "Too late for that now."

"Thank you, for taking care of me." I look over at Holly to see her staring at me with puppylike eyes, wide and adorable.

"Of course," I tell her.

"You didn't have to. Gran would have, or even Tally." Both of whom had stayed home once they realized Holly was sick, but they've been pretty hands off and let me take care of her.

"I know."

"But you still did." She's eyeing me curiously now and the unsaid words hang between us. *You still did even though none of this is real.*

I swallow. "We're friends, aren't we?"

Holly nods slowly in response and grabs another cracker. "Still, thank you."

"Anytime," I tell her, realizing I actually mean it.

It's after seven and I'm still in Holly's bed. Tally and Gran left a bit ago to attend the rehearsal dinner, assuring Holly that her dad was okay with her not coming and only hopes she'll be feeling better soon. I'm thankful for a quiet evening without everyone in her family in the house. I'm going to need all of next week to recover from this one.

Holly is awake but has her head on my chest as we watch another one of her favorite romance movies on her laptop—I've already forgotten the name of this one. I think the first one we watched was called *While You Were Sleeping*. I guess I finally understand what it means for a guy to lean, though I'm not sure I've ever done that in my entire life. Right now, I'm not even watching the movie. Instead, I'm focused on keeping my hands where they are and not moving them. One is around her back, tucking her in close to me and the other is in my lap, inches from Holly's own hand.

The main characters in the movie have just confessed they have feelings for one another when Holly sits up slightly, still in my arms.

"Is this..." she pauses, looking me dead in the eye, and gestures to the two of us. "Giving the wrong impression?"

I want to ask her why it matters and why she thinks it would be giving the wrong impression. I want to tell her that of course it's not giving the wrong impression because it's all fake, even if my brain is going haywire. Instead, I give her a teasing smile and pull her back against my chest. "You mean the cuddling?"

I feel more than hear Holly's groan against my chest. "I just don't want to give the wrong idea."

Oof. That's like a knife straight to my heart. I remind myself that I shouldn't care so much—that I can't care so much—because all of this is fake anyway.

"The only way it would give me the wrong idea is if you did this." With my free hand, I find hers and lace our fingers together for a moment. We both stare at our entwined hands for a second before I pull away. "But since we're not doing that, no confusion."

Holly sits up again and nods. Now that I can see her face, I wonder what she's thinking because part of her brow is furrowed and I want to take my thumb and smooth it out.

"You okay?" I grab the puke bowl and try to give it to her. She shakes her head and pushes it away.

"I'm fine," Holly says but she doesn't meet my eye. A moment later, she's tucked back into my side, her head on my chest and watching the movie again.

A few minutes go by before I feel it—a feather light touch on the palm of my hand in my lap. My breath catches, but I force myself to breathe and to not look away from the screen. I imagined the touch, there's no way she actually touched me like that on purpose.

I focus on breathing in and out like I'm in the middle of one of those meditations I hate, but I don't want her to see how her probably accidental touch did anything to me. In...out... I can do this. I'm fine. Totally fine.

Until she touches my hand again, and this time I know it wasn't an accident. Her fingers are still featherlike, but now they trace the lines on the palm of my hand and I'm mesmerized. I can't look away. I don't have it in me to look away. I watch as she traces the lines again and again, each time getting closer to threading her fingers with mine.

Did she not hear what I just said? That all of this was fine—enough anyway—unless she held my hand. If she did that, then I don't know what to think. But all I can focus on right now is keeping my breathing normal, even though that's freaking hard because of the warmth that seems to be spreading through my entire body.

My breath catches—and I can tell she notices, because she freezes for a split second—when she threads her fingers through mine, just like it was a moment ago, only this time, it's not for show. And I don't know what that means.

But Holly doesn't move to look up at me, she is still facing the laptop and her breathing is perfectly even, so I count to ten and focus on breathing again, even though the only thing my brain can think about is the fact that she's holding my hand, and that she held it on purpose right after I told her that it was the only thing that would make this confusing.

I try to focus on how it feels to hold her. Her small frame tucked into mine, our hands intertwined. And...I don't hate it. Actually, I really like it and I never want to move.

HOLLY

Rule #16: He has to care deeply about life, other people, and me

I HAVE no idea how my heart isn't beating out of my chest right now. Any time a guy has ever tried to hold my hand before, immediately my heart rate spikes and I start sweating like I'm standing in the desert sun, and not simply holding a man's hand. And I'm the one that made the move to hold Drew's hand. I've never done anything like this before. I've never been so forward in my life and I don't know what compelled me to grab his hand in the first place. I just couldn't get what he'd said out of my head, how if I was holding his hand that would be confusing since this is fake.

And it is. This is crazy confusing.

I'm not the type of woman who does this. I don't flirt or tease or lead men along. Probably because it has never even gotten far enough along to do those things in the first place.

But right now, I'm snuggled up against my *fake* boyfriend and I'm holding his hand.

I don't even know what it means that I chose to hold his hand when I did, I just know that I was curious about how it would feel. For a moment, I wanted to pretend that he was actually my boyfriend and not just a friend who'd spent the day taking care of me. What would it feel like to hold his hand? I hadn't been able to get the thought out of my head and so, I just did it.

But now that I'm here, listening to his steady heart rate—seriously, how is this not affecting his breathing at all? I realize that I might have made a mistake.

Because if he feels absolutely nothing, then I just shot my shot and it was incredibly stupid. He's supposed to be helping me get ready to date Jim when we get back home.

Jim. The man I've been "in love with" for three years yet have never even talked to about something not school related without making a complete fool of myself. Jim. The man who hasn't even crossed my mind since our first day here.

Wait.

He hasn't? Huh.

I replay the past few days in my mind and I don't know exactly when the shift happened—if it was before or after my kiss with Drew—that I had stopped thinking about Jim and started thinking about Drew. It was so subtle I hadn't even noticed.

Which is a problem, because now I'm sitting here *holding Drew's hand* and that might mean something I'm not ready to admit. But I don't pull away.

As if reading my thoughts, Drew shifts slightly, but doesn't pull away either. Instead, he moves his thumb slowly over the back of my hand. I watch, mesmerized.

I have to do something, because if I don't say anything, I'm afraid he'll bolt. "Thanks for being here this week. It's always a hard week, without my mom, but having you here has helped.

I'm glad we're friends." Yeah. Sure. Friends who hold hands and then ignore that...oops.

"You're welcome," Drew says, his voice is even and normal. I should pull my hand away, this obviously isn't doing anything to him. This was a mistake. "Tell me about your mom, why did she love this week so much?"

My heart constricts in my chest. I feel a wave of grief and gratitude all rolled into one. It's really hard to not have Mom here, but I also love talking about her. "She made this week of the year so magical. I swear she was trying to convince Tally and I that Santa was still real, up until the year she died. We were both adults by that point, but I really think she didn't want us to lose any of the magic that came with the Christmas traditions. So many of my holiday sweaters I got from her, and I love wearing them because it feels like I get to carry her with me. She's gone, but it's like part of her is still here. Does that make sense?"

"Yeah," Drew says and I wonder if he means it. "I'm sorry you lost her."

"Thanks," I say. "And you really didn't ever have any holiday traditions growing up?" My heart hurts for him if it's true. I can't imagine not having a good childhood. I'm not naive enough to think that everyone had a childhood like mine—with a family who loved and cared for me and did things together. But it still baffles me that people would bring children into the world only to neglect and ignore them.

"Nope," Drew answers, his voice oddly stiff. "I was too busy trying to keep Leo out of trouble to worry about Christmas or any other holidays."

"That must have been hard," I say and we fall into a quiet, comfortable silence.

Then, without warning, Drew pulls away and moves quickly off the bed and runs his hands through his hair before looking at me with bleary and wide eyes. "We probably shouldn't."

I sit straight up, and my head spins. I'm still weak from being sick all day, even if I feel a thousand times better. "Right. I'm sorry. I wasn't thinking."

Drew looks at me then, and his gaze nearly makes my heart stop. He's staring at me the way the hero always stares at the love interest in movies, like he's afraid of how much he loves her. I want to ask him why he's looking at me like that—as if I just stole his puppy or broke his heart—when *he* was the one that pulled away. But the words get stuck in my throat.

I held his hand and he pulled away. Shame fills my body. Of course, he didn't mean anything when he said that it would make things confusing if I held his hand. Of course, he doesn't actually feel anything for me, I'm stuck in fantasy land in my mind, just like I usually am. I can't believe I let myself kind of start to fall for him, he's just the guy that's here right now, that's been flirting with me in front of my family and who gave me the best first kiss ever. But it doesn't mean anything. Why would it? He's made it abundantly clear up to this point in our acquaintanceship that he doesn't do relationships, ever. Now I know why, with his history about his brother and his ex, but did I really believe that I could be the exception?

"It's okay." Drew brushes off my comment and I notice him take a half step toward the door. "I think you just need more rest; you were sick all day. Get some sleep. Okay?"

"Okay." I watch as he leaves the room in a rush. I slump against the pillows, the smell of Drew surrounds me thanks to him being in my bed all day with me, and I wipe away a single tear before it gets the chance to fall.

I will not cry over him. Our relationship isn't even real.

There's a quiet knock on my door before it swings open and Tally walks in. "How are you feeling today?"

"Better than yesterday," I tell her honestly as I slowly sit up. "At least physically."

Her brow furrows but I shake my head, not ready to talk about my not fake feelings for Drew and how I made a complete fool of myself. She doesn't ask me to elaborate and I'm thankful.

"Noah and I have the day off today, since it's Christmas Eve and the shop is closed until the new year. So Drew and I were thinking that if you're up for it, before the wedding we could do some of the things he had planned for yesterday."

My nose scrunches at the mention of the wedding, but I can worry about that later. I don't have to think about it in this moment.

"Drew and you were thinking that?" I ask Tally instead.

"Yeah, we just talked about it in the kitchen."

"Was it your idea or his?" I ask her, because if it was her idea and he's just going along with it, there's no way I'm getting out of this bed.

"His. He asked if we had anything planned today, and we don't have anything except the wedding tonight, and Dad paid out for everything so no one has to do anything but show up. So, you won't get your party, but we can still have a fun day since our usual Christmas Eve traditions aren't happening."

I keep my breathing even and try not to let my mind race. Everything about this day feels like a lot, and I can't spend the entire day wondering whether or not he actually likes me. I'm an adult, I can be an adult about this. Plus, going out and having fun might keep my brain distracted from everything that I'm trying not to think about. "That's okay, that sounds fun. What has Drew got planned?"

Tally shakes her head. "Uh-huh. I'm not telling. Just get ready and wear something warm, we'll be outside for part of today."

I hold back a groan. There was a time in my life where I loved to be outside in the winter, I loved the snow and the cold, but since living in California, most of the cold just gets on my nerves. I force myself to smile. "Sounds interesting."

And it does, because what on earth could we be doing that will make us spend any time outside?

I stretch and stand slowly, waiting for the nausea to hit again like it did any time I moved yesterday. Whatever sort of bug I caught, I'm glad it was quick and that it's over now. My stomach growls and Tally laughs.

"I'll make you some toast and then we can get ready to leave. Noah's already on his way over."

"Great," I say, feeling only slightly less enthusiastic than I probably should. Sure, I spent my birthday sick in bed, but now I get a do-over, shouldn't I be thrilled about that?

Thirty minutes later, we pile into Noah's car. Tally scrolls through his phone to find some music to listen to—instead of the romance novel that started playing as soon as we got in—and Drew holds my hand across the middle seat. I want to pull away, but Drew doesn't know that Tally (and probably Noah, because let's be honest, she probably told him) knows it's all fake. But I can't exactly announce that to the car without making everything feel more awkward than it already does.

So, we hold hands as I stare out the window and we head up the canyon. I try very hard not to think about how his hand feels against mine, how every time he occasionally brushes his thumb against the back of my hand I have to suppress a shiver. And at this point I don't trust myself to know if what I'm feeling is real, or if I'm only feeling this way because I've never dated a guy before.

I know where we're going before we pull in, and it takes everything in me to get out of the car without feeling emotional. I shove down the grief that threatens to burst when I see Tally's smiling face and Drew watching me expectantly.

"Surprise!" Tally says, throwing her arms in the air and gesturing toward the ice castles that are here in Midway every year.

The last time I came here was the birthday before my mom died. It was a thing we used to do every year, usually just the two of us, but sometimes Tally came too. But every year, on my birthday, we came here.

I stopped coming after she was gone because it hurt too much to come here without her. Tally knows that, she has to know that.

"Wow," I manage to say. Drew steps closer to me.

"Are you alright?" He asks so quietly that I can't tell if Tally and Noah actually can't hear or if they are simply pretending not to notice.

I swallow the lump in my throat. "I used to come here with my mom."

A mix of emotions flash across Drew's face as he tries to figure out what to say. "We can go do something else, Tally suggested it and I thought it would be fun and maybe a good photo opportunity." He holds up his camera that I just now realize he's wearing around his neck. "But we can go."

I look up at him and his expression is full of genuine care and concern. "We can stay." I take a deep breath. "I want to stay."

"You're sure?" Drew asks, watching me intently.

I nod. "Yeah, I'm sure." I take the first step toward the entrance, the snow on the ground crunching under my boots. I'm taken back in time, back to when Mom and I used to come here every year. But it's not only that. I feel like I do every time I do something for the first time without her, it hits me straight in the heart. I don't notice it as much these days, since so much of my life is routine. I don't go out and do new things often and the things I do now that she used to love, I've done a thousand times since she passed so they don't hurt as much now.

I forgot what it was like to do something for the first time—something we used to do together—without her. I wish she was here.

But my eyes stay dry as we pay to get in and as we walk inside one of the ice castles. They are just as stunning as I remember. The ice is purple and pink and blue, and reflects the sun as we make our way around the different areas. My artist's eye loves it, and being here feels like I'm close to Mom too. I shouldn't have stayed away for so long. Coming here today was the best possible thing that could have happened because I feel her here, and I was worried I wouldn't feel her today. I needed this.

I'm staring at the ice when I hear a camera click and I whirl to see Drew facing me, camera raised, lens pointing at me. "I'll make sure you get a copy of that one," he says before looking around more. "This place is incredible."

"It is, isn't it?" I ask and we smile when we make eye contact again. The awkwardness from last night melts away, at least for this moment. I'm glad we're friends and I'm glad we're experiencing this together.

chapter 22

DREW

"DO you think we could take some pictures today?" Tally asks me from the front seat. "I'll pay you, but the snow is just so pretty and I'd love some pictures of us in the snow."

"Sure," I tell her. It's been too long since I've taken photos of people—couples specifically—but I'm beginning to feel like I'd do just about anything for Holly and her family. "You'll have to find a good spot, since I'm not familiar with the area."

I glance over at Holly, but she's staring out the window again. She's been quiet most of the morning. I know part of it is my fault. Maybe I shouldn't have pulled away last night, but it seemed like the right thing to do in the moment. I shouldn't be giving her any ideas. I can be her friend—her friend that's starting to fall for her—but not anything more. That's what we both need right now more than anything else.

"You alright with that?" I reach out and touch Holly's shoulder, and she jumps as if she's a million miles away and not right here in the car with us.

"Yup," she says, even though I'm fairly certain she has no idea what we're talking about.

A few minutes later, Noah pulls his car off into an empty

parking lot with a nearly pristine white field full of snow-covered trees. "This will be perfect."

I haven't done a couples shoot in so long, but Noah and Tally are easy to photograph. They're so in love, I don't even have to give them any directions because they're just naturally talking, laughing, and posing.

"Do you think we can get some of these printed before tomorrow?" Tally asks as she looks over my shoulder at my camera. "I'd love to have them for Christmas."

"Possibly. We can try anyway," I tell her. "If not, everything should be open again the day after Christmas."

"Okay, now we need to get some of the two of you," Noah says, gesturing between me and Holly.

"What?" Holly's eyes are wide.

"Come on, the two of you are adorable," Noah says and I bite my lip to hold back my rude remark. "Show me what to do."

I keep the shutter speed the same as before and tell Noah that all he needs to do is point the camera and click. It's more complicated than that, really, but for this it will be fine.

I grab Holly's hand and we make our own path in the snow to a smaller clearing between some snow-covered pine trees.

"What do I do now?" Holly asks, her arms awkwardly by her side. I pull our intertwined hands up to my chest and look down at her.

"Look at me like you're in love with me," I tell her, and when her cheeks turn pink I know it's not from the cold.

The smile I give her is real. Not that any of the smiles I've given her for the past four days haven't been real, but this one means something. Holly blinks once as she stares up at me and then gives me a tentative smile as well. I let go of her hand and pull her against me in a hug.

I feel her catch her breath as she turns her head toward the camera. I lift her slightly, and try to spin. But my shoes—which are not built for the snow—slip and I fall to the ground, pulling Holly on top of me.

"Ooof," I groan. I'm going to need an ice bath or a hot tub tonight. My back already hurts.

"Oh my gosh!" Holly pushes herself up, hands on my chest, so she can look down and inspect me. "Are you okay?"

Our eyes meet as her hair cascades around us. The grin on her face is so childlike and pure, like she's trying to smother a laugh. I've still got my arms around her, holding her to me.

"Fine," I get out once I catch my breath. "Just got the wind knocked out of me."

"Snow can be slippery," Holly giggles. "I should have warned you, Mr. California."

I raise my eyebrows at her. "Mr. California?"

"What?" Holly leans back a little so our faces aren't so close. "I'm still trying to come up with a good nickname for you. And you clearly don't have any snow shoes."

"This wasn't on the agenda," I tell her as I hear a camera click from somewhere up above us.

"But tubing is!" Tally calls from my right.

Holly can't hold back her laugh after that. It's a deep belly laugh, one that I feel through my whole body and not just because she's lying on top of me. The smile reaches her eyes and it's the most beautiful thing I've ever seen. "Come on, Mr. Slip 'n Slide, let's get up before you get soaked." Holly rolls off of me and stands, brushing the snow off her pants and then reaches out her hand to help me up.

I don't let myself look at the photos of Holly and I when we get back to the car. I already know that I'm not ready to see the expression that was on my face the whole time I had my arms around her. Because I'm fairly certain I look like a lovesick fool, which is ridiculous, because all of this is supposed to be fake anyway. I'm not supposed to actually have feelings for her.

But she held your hand last night. The memory hits me hard and once it's back in my brain, I can't get rid of it.

Our next stop is a quick lunch and then after, we head to our last stop of the day: tubing—I just found out this week it's basically sledding but in a giant tube instead of on a sled. Not that I've ever gone sledding before. I grew up in Southern California, we didn't go sledding, or anywhere for that matter.

"Nervous?" Holly asks once we have our double tube and make our way to the line where we'll get strapped in and pulled up to the top.

Can she tell that I'm slightly jittery? "Um, a little."

She punches me lightly on the shoulder, and it's cold enough that I can see her breath when she talks. "It'll be fun. It's kind of like a rush the first time, and the second, and the thirteenth."

"Comforting," I smile at her.

"And because you're bigger than me, you get to hold onto my legs so that I don't fall out."

I don't know if she's being serious or joking about that, so I simply nod in response. When we get to the bottom of the hill, where a worker hooks a small rope on our tube to the pully system that will pull us up the hill, he tells me to sit in front and sure enough, Holly tucks her legs under my arms and then we're off.

"Which hill should we go down first?" Holly asks once we get to the top. There are several different ways down that we can pick from.

"The smoothest, less scary one?" I ask her but she's already grinning and my stomach swirls at what's about to happen.

"How about that one?" She points to the one with the

longest line, and a sign that says 'jump ahead'. I nearly gulp. I never would have pegged Holly for being the gutsy one out of the two of us, but here we are.

"Okay." Even though I've been going back and forth all day, reminding myself why it's such a bad idea to get involved with anyone—especially her—I can't seem to help it. I'd follow her anywhere. And no matter what happens when we get back to California, I hope we stay friends. Something I never thought I'd say about anyone again.

Holly's smile lights up the world and makes my chest feel warm. Saying yes was definitely the right choice. Even if I regret it the moment it's our turn. We take our places in the tube, the worker instructing us to hold on so we don't go flying after the jump and to keep our butts slightly lifted so they don't slam into the ground when we land. Comforting. Before I can change my mind, he pushes us down the hill.

The scream that comes out of me is high and loud, and I can hear Holly laughing behind me. We hit the jump and then we're in the air.

It's pure exhilaration.

I groan a bit when we hit the ground again and continue to slide down the mountain.

As we come to a stop, I'm grinning. I hop out of the tube and grab Holly's hand to help her up. She wraps her arms around me and time stops.

"Wasn't that fun!?" She asks, her eyes are sparkling like the snow and I have to kiss her. I need to kiss her.

My arms go around her waist. "Very fun, Holly."

My voice is gruff and Holly glances at my lips when I say her name. That's all it takes before I lift her higher and pull her to me. Her lips are just as soft as they were the first time we kissed, only this time, it's not for show. I hear a tube whip past us and part of my brain realizes that standing here, at the bottom of the hill is probably not the smartest idea, but I don't care.

All I care about right now is the fact that I am kissing Holly Nelson, and she's kissing me back. I'm tempted to taste her lips with my tongue, but I keep my lips closed. Now is not the time or place to make out—this is a family establishment after all. I've seen at least a hundred kids and teenagers since we got here. I deepen the kiss though, by slowing my lips and I feel Holly's fingers in my hair.

Before I want to, I pull away, slowly, and ease Holly back onto her feet.

"Ready to do that again?" She asks, her eyes still shining. I know she's talking about tubing, but my mind will never erase that kiss.

Our first real kiss.

"Always."

Holly holds out her hand and I grab it with one of mine, pulling our tube behind us with the other.

chapter 23

HOLLY

Rule #20: He needs to be romantic

I HAVE time for a quick nap when we get back to Grans, and I stay in bed longer than I should. I need to get ready for the wedding, but it feels weird to be getting ready for such a busy evening when this day usually holds so much peace and joy for me.

Plus, I can't stop thinking about that kiss. Drew kissed me, like really kissed me. I touch my lips and feel the ghost of his there. I lean back on my pillow, letting out a sigh. I probably shouldn't, but I really hope he'll kiss me again tonight.

There's a soft knock on my door. "Come in," I call, expecting it to be Drew or Tally on the other side. I'm surprised when Dad is the one that walks in.

"Hey, sweetheart," he says as he shuts the door quietly behind him. "Can we talk for a minute?"

I nod. It's been so long since Dad and I had any sort of real conversation—one that went beyond how we're doing on the surface and the day-to-day things that happen for both of us.

Dad sits on the edge of my bed and I pull the covers up to my chin.

"I know tonight is going to be full of different emotions," Dad starts and I take a sharp breath. "It's Mom's favorite day, and yours."

My eyes start to water. It feels impossible that we're having this conversation. When he told me he was going to get married on Christmas Eve, it felt like someone was squeezing my insides and wouldn't let go. I couldn't catch a breath. Over and over, I've been pushing the thought out of my mind that Dad doesn't care, because he has to care, even if he hadn't said anything. But he's saying something now.

"I should have explained better why we picked today." Dad's eyes meet mine and he gives me a soft, sad sort of smile when he sees the tears in them. He puts a hand on my leg, over the covers and starts to talk. "For the past six years, today has been the hardest day of my life. Harder even than your mom's birthday or the anniversary of her death."

I nod, because in some ways, that's been true for me too. It only felt okay the past few years because we did the same things we always did when she was here and that felt a little like we were keeping her with us. Doing something different—which I knew we would be as soon as Dad told me about his wedding plans—feels like the biggest sort of betrayal. And not really even because he is getting married again—I know she would have hoped that he'd find love again—but because today was her day in so many ways. I'm grateful for the moment I felt close to her, when we were at the ice castles, but that doesn't really make any of this easier.

Dad takes a deep breath. "I don't know if you've noticed, not that it's your job as my daughter to do that, but the past few years on Christmas Eve, I've retreated to the edges. While you and Tally and everyone else have been able to feel close to Mom by doing what we've always done, it seemed to crack the hole inside my heart just a little bit wider with every tradition, every present and song and memory that we did without her."

A tear falls, and I don't move to wipe it away. I felt that way too, at least the first few years I did. Now that feeling creeps in, but it doesn't linger like it did back then. The first Christmas I felt happy after she was gone felt weirdly like a betrayal to her, but also a way to honor her. Because she would have wanted us to enjoy the day. She would have wanted us to be happy doing the things we've always all loved. For the past couple of years, it hasn't felt so much like pretending for me, even though I'd give anything to have her back with us.

"I know that you were always thinking about her." Dad smiles a bit like he's about to chuckle. "That's the funny thing about grief, it feels and shows up differently in all of us."

I sniff. "That's true."

Dad reaches out and I pull an arm out from under the covers so he can hold my hand. Just then the door opens and Tally walks in. "Gran said you were here."

Dad simply nods and pats the open space beside him on the bed. Tally sits, tucking her legs under her. "I was just telling Holly why Beth and I picked today."

Tally lays her head on his shoulder in response and I wonder if they've already had this conversation, since she sees him more often in person.

"When Beth and I started thinking about when we wanted to get married, she kept coming back to today. At first, I was angry. She knew what this day meant to me and to all of us, and I couldn't believe that she would even suggest it. Then she explained that she hated seeing me so sad and down on Christmas Eve every year. She knew that nothing would probably ever change that, that it would always be a hard day. But she explained that if we get married today, then maybe there would be a reason for joy to co-exist with the grief."

We're all crying now.

"I thought about it for a long time and one night I woke up out of the blue and it felt almost like your mother had been there, just on the edges of my dream, telling me that I should do it. That I should let the joy and grief co-exist a little better in my life. That she'd want this for me. The next morning, I told Beth and here we are."

After Dad finishes talking, we're all quiet in our own thoughts. I'm thankful he doesn't expect me to talk right now, because even though now I understand a little more why he picked today of all days, I still can't find my voice.

"How are things with Drew?" Dad asks, filling the silence and changing the subject. I try to think of a good way to answer that question, because I don't actually know. Then Dad surprises me. "Tally told me the truth. You could have told me Holls, I can take it. You don't have to pretend for me, I just want you to be happy."

I glance at Tally who looks sheepish.

Dad continues. "I will say that when Tally told me it was all fake, I didn't believe it. I still don't. And you might think it's fake, but anyone with eyes would tell you that what Drew feels for you is not fake."

My face flushes as I remember earlier this afternoon. A switch was flipped and everything changed after we kissed. We laughed and flirted, and he kissed me one more time, just before we headed back home after one of the best days of my life. "I don't think it's fake for me either."

"Good." Dad squeezes my hand. "I can tell he really cares about you by the way he looks at you."

"Dad," I groan. Maybe this wouldn't be so embarrassing if we'd had conversations like this when I was younger, but I feel like a teenager right now instead of a woman who's a year closer to thirty.

Dad just smiles at me. "I've got a good feeling about him." And for the first time this week, I do too. Because something real happened today and I don't think there's any going back. At least not for me.

Dad's wedding is beautiful, but I can't really say that I'm fully present for all of it. Somehow, I make it from the wedding to the small reception hall where the dinner and dancing will be held.

The venue for the wedding is stunning, but my mind is elsewhere. My heart is with Mom and our usual traditions. Dad is glowing, and I am happy for him, and while I'm grateful he explained his reasoning for picking this day to get married, it doesn't make it easier.

I catch Drew's eyes as he makes his way across the room toward our table. A zing goes through my entire body, and it's like it's only me and him in the room, like there is some sort of magnetic pull between the two of us.

"You alright?" Drew slides into the seat beside me, his arm going around the back of my chair, fingers gently touching my back.

"Mostly," I tell him because I've already been emotionally vulnerable today. I'm not ready to have another deep conversation about my feelings.

"Anything I can do?" Drew asks, and his eyes are so soft and gentle as he looks at me, it makes me melt a little inside.

"Dance with me?" The dance floor is empty, since no one has even had food yet. There's soft music playing over the speaker and Drew stands, holding out a hand.

"Always."

I smile up at him as I slip my hand in his. I'm grateful he's here and that I didn't have to do today alone. Not that I would have been completely alone if he hadn't been here, I still would have had Gran who cried nearly the entire ceremony and Tally who's been making heart eyes at Noah all evening—probably daydreaming about her own wedding since she's been engaged for a month.

I'm surrounded by cousins and aunts and uncles, just like every Christmas Eve, but it still feels different because it is different. My heart aches a little at the thought of it. It's only for this year, I remind myself. Next year, everything will go back to normal. Everything will be the same as it always is on Christmas Eve. A day spent with family, but at Gran's house.

Drew stops in the middle of the dance floor, an arm wrapping around my waist, pulling me back to the present moment. He looks so good tonight, in a dress shirt and a deep green tie that matches the dress that Tally picked out for me. His hair is brushed back, out of his eyes and it looks like he trimmed his beard.

I'm already itching to kiss him again. He hasn't tried to kiss me, not since we got back to Gran's, but I really want him too. I think he can sense my nerves about the wedding though, and as much as I want to distract myself by kissing him again, I'm grateful he's dancing with me.

The song playing is a slow one and we rock side to side. I've got one hand on Drew's chest and he's got the other cradled in his hand, with his other hand low on my back. For one blissful moment, I forget that it's Christmas Eve. I forget that we should be heading to Gran's right now for food and games and to watch the little kids act out the nativity story.

I forget that there are conversations we need to have about how this is going to work when we get home.

I'm simply here in this moment. Drew's arm around me,

holding me close to him. Gingerly, I lay my head against his chest and listen to his heart beating, nearly as fast as my own. And I smile, because this moment might just make one of my favorite Christmas Eve memories ever, and it's not even over yet. It hits me that while everything about today has been different than what I expected and wanted, it's still been incredible.

"So." I look up at Drew and he pulls me a tiny bit closer to him. "What is this? This thing between us. Does it end when we get back to California?"

I don't know where my bravery is coming from. All I know is that he's not like anything I expected—he's better—and I keep on falling for him. I need to know if he's feeling the same way.

"I hope not." Drew smiles down at me. He seems so different than just a few days ago, back when he was swearing off any type of real relationship. I understand why, but it still makes my heart skip a beat the way he's looking at me. Like he cares. Like he wants me to be his.

I grin up at him.

Drew leans down and presses a gentle kiss against my lips just as the song ends. Taking my hand, he leads me back to the table for a drink of water. My dad and Beth are still out on the dance floor, and Tally and Noah as well. I didn't even realize they had started dancing. I sink into my chair, feeling exhausted and elated all at once.

Then my phone lights up on the table and time seems to slow down.

I've had Jim's phone number saved in my phone, purely for school related reasons, but I've never had to use it and he's never sent me a text. But now there's one shining up for Drew and I to both see. I feel Drew tense beside me as we both read the words. He isn't even trying to be subtle about reading my text and I should be mad, but all I feel is dread.

JIM SULLIVAN

Hey Holly. Drew Rossi texted me earlier this week, saying that he thought you and I would be a good fit. I know it's not great practice to ask someone out on a date over text, but I won't be back to California for another week and I can't stop thinking about it. Can I take you out on New Year's Eve? A buddy of mine is hosting a party and I'd love for you to be my date.

I stare at the words. A week ago, I would have died and gone to heaven to see this text staring up at me from my screen. But now I want to take my phone and delete the message. Instead, I simply flip my phone over and avoid looking at Drew. Can I really like this man that I've spent barely a week with? Can this really be the beginning of something new or am I rushing it because he's been here and he's the first guy I've ever done anything romantic with, even though it started out as fake?

Drew's warm hand slips into mine. "You can say yes, if you want."

"What?" I look up at him, trying to read his face, but he's got a mask over his emotions and I have no idea what he's actually thinking.

"That was the whole point of this, wasn't it?" Drew rubs his beard thoughtfully with his other hand.

"But you just said..." I think back to literally minutes ago on the dance floor.

"I know." Drew's eyes meet mine. "All I'm saying is that if you still want to go out with him, you should."

Is this Drew's way of telling me he's not actually committed to me? That he wants an out but was caught up in the moment a few minutes ago and that's why he said what he did? Because the Drew I'm looking at now isn't looking at me with his shining, nearly lovesick eyes like he has been all day. He's back to the old Drew, the one with the hard mask on all the time.

"And if I don't want to go out with him anymore? What then?" I ask him, just to see what he says.

"I just want you to be sure that this is what you want." Drew searches my face, but I can tell his mask is still up and that annoys me. I know it's only been less than a week for us, but there's obviously something here, can't he see that? Doesn't he know that? Maybe I shouldn't have let so many of my rules slide. I should have remembered them to keep myself from falling for him, if he doesn't even trust me.

I nod. "I want to see where this goes, with you and me." I hold up our intertwined hands between us. I'm taking a leap, one that I don't know if he'll actually want to take with me, even with what he said while we were dancing. Especially with how he's looking at me, but for the first time in my life I want to be brave, even if it means throwing out so many of my rules.

Drew lets out what I think is a hesitant sigh. "Then we'll see where this goes."

chapter 24

HOLLY

Rule #18: He has to love Christmas

"YOU'VE BEEN quiet on the way home, everything okay?" I
ask Drew as we pull up to Gran's house after the wedding. I
wish I could say that it was a day I'd always remember, that the
wedding has been seared into my brain, but I kind of feel the
opposite. And I feel bad about it. It was such a special day for
Dad and the only things that stand out from today have been the
conversation I had with Dad earlier and Drew kissing me.

Do all first real kisses take over your brain like that? It's like I
can't stop replaying the moment in my head. I knew before it
happened, I could tell from the look on Drew's face that he was
going to kiss me and that it was going to be for real. And then he
did and it was as if no one else in the world existed but me and
him. I want to spend the rest of forever kissing him, but I keep
pushing that thought away, no need to get completely carried
away here.

But today was the first day where we weren't pretending. I
wasn't worried about what my family would think or if I was

doing enough to make our relationship seem believable. Because every glance, every lingering touch, it was all real.

At least until Jim texted. And while Drew said he wants to see what happens with us, he's been quiet ever since.

"Just tired," Drew answers, but I'm not sure I believe him.

I give his arm a squeeze before resting my head on his shoulder as Gran pulls into the garage. "Well, we've still got a few things to do tonight."

"I thought the wedding meant your usual traditions weren't happening," Drew murmurs against my hair. I close my eyes and relish in his closeness. I need to stop worrying about the future—whether there is one for us or not—and just enjoy these moments that I do get to have with him.

I shake my head. "Well, kind of. All the big family stuff isn't happening this year, like dinner and the younger kids acting out the nativity story, since we were with everyone all evening. But the night is still young."

"What else are we doing?" Drew asks.

Gran is the one who replies. "I've got a present for each of you. Once you get changed, we'll take pictures."

"Changed?" Drew asks.

"You'll see," I tell him. I guessed his size for the Christmas pajamas that Gran gets us every year. It was something she started doing with Tally and I after Mom died, since it was a tradition that Mom always did with Dad, but he couldn't do it that first year after Mom was gone, so Gran stepped in. Mom always went a little bit overboard and got the pajamas that screamed Christmas, but I have to admit that somehow Gran is the queen at finding the wildest and funniest Christmas pajamas out there.

I can't wait to see what mine looks like this year.

Once we're inside, Gran hands Drew and I our presents

along with Tally and Noah—he's spending the night on the couch to be here on Christmas morning.

I hold up my present to Drew as if holding up a glass of champagne. "See you in a bit." Drew lifts his package, clearly confused, and heads to his room.

Once in my own room, I open the present and start laughing. "You would, Gran." This year she's picked a deep blue onesie covered with little Santa faces all over it.

I slip out of the velvet dress from the wedding and pull on the fuzzy onesie. It fits perfectly, just like always. Gran is also the queen of sizes, so I hope whatever she got for Drew fits him.

My covered feet are muffled in the hallway as I walk out toward the Christmas tree. Sitting down on the ground I stare up at the twinkling rainbow lights and ornaments I've grown to love over the years. I wrap my arms around my middle, taking it all in.

I haven't had a chance to catch my breath today, and looking at the tree that was a part of every single Christmas growing up gives me a knot in my throat. Will I ever get over things being different from when I was little? Will it always hurt so much, knowing that every year it's another Christmas without Mom? I hug my arms tighter around myself, as if I can squeeze out my own pain.

"You look like you're trying to cling to something that's about to slip away," Drew whispers into my ear as he sits behind me, his arms coming around me in a protective hug. I lean into the warmth.

I nod, not trusting my voice.

"Sometimes we have to let things go, so that we can live in the moment. And some things you need to hold onto, at least in your heart," Drew says but he tightens his grip around me. "I've got you, though. Right now, I've got you."

I lean my head against his chest and breathe in his familiar minty fresh and pine scent. I closed my eyes and let his words soak in, hoping that one day I will believe them.

"Nice onesie by the way," Drew says and I can hear the smile in his voice.

Blinking away my tears, I glance back at him and I can't hold back my laugh. "We're twins."

There are not many sights I'd pay money to see. I get to see the ocean every single day and nothing gets better than watching the sun set over the water, but seeing the deep blue onesie hug Drew's arms and body makes me wonder if maybe there's more to life than painting pretty sunsets.

"That we are." Drew chuckles, then he leans in and presses a kiss against my cheek.

"Picture time! Then bed," Gran hollers as she comes into the room. "I'm tired."

Drew releases me and we both get up off the floor. Tally is laughing as she comes up the stairs with Noah, who are also in matching onesies, theirs are red with little reindeers all over.

We take a few silly pictures standing in front of the Christmas tree. Then Gran says we need a few of just Drew and I. "Well kiss her why don't you, I know you've been wanting to all day," Gran says and I see Tally raise an eyebrow. I haven't had a chance to tell her that things changed from when we first got here, that things are real now and it's not fake at all anymore. The feelings are real. Tally missed our kiss earlier too. There's so much I need to tell her, but there just hasn't been any time.

Drew, however, doesn't need to be told twice before he's already pulling me to him. His lips brush mine and he pulls away before I even have a chance to process that he's kissed me again. Dread fills my belly. Is this how all relationships work? You always want more until you don't and someone inevitably breaks the other person's heart? I lick my lips and smile up at him so that he can't see my thoughts on my face.

This week has been magical, but very different than our regular life. Will we even make it in the real world? What on earth was I thinking, bringing him along to pretend to be my boyfriend and then actually falling for him? Everything was safer when I was in love with Jim and no one actually knew that.

"You alright?" Drew furrows his brow at me. Apparently, he can already see through my forced smile.

"Just tired." It's not a lie, just not the whole truth. "It's been quite the day."

 *chapter 25*

DREW

IT'S way too early the next morning when I feel the bed shift beside me. A second ago, someone—Holly—flipped on the light and said "Merry Christmas" way too cheerfully for someone who hates mornings.

I pulled the covers over my head, which is where I am still hiding.

"Come on, Mr. Sleepyhead." Holly pokes me through the covers. "It's time for presents."

"Too early," I grumble. Every day of the year I get up before five so I can run. The only day I don't run is Christmas and I don't even like Christmas that much, but it felt like a good holiday to give myself a break. It's like a Christmas present to myself of sorts.

"Do I need to start a tickle fight?" Holly asks in a sing-song voice and even though I am kind of grumpy for being woken up early on the only day of the year I let myself sleep in, I peek an eye out.

"Do. Not. Tickle. Me."

She raises her eyebrows over her glasses. "Hmm. I think that means I need to." Her hand moves toward me and I try to wrap the blanket that's already around me tighter, but she finds an opening and then her freezing cold fingers are on my skin.

Her hand stills and her eyes go wide.

We may have decided to see where things go with us, but I still need to move slow with Holly. She's never been in a relationship before, I'm not about to do anything that truly makes her uncomfortable. Plus, I know I need to move slowly to protect both our hearts.

But, teasing her is always fun.

"Like what you feel?" I give her a lazy grin and she tries to pull her hand away, a move I was anticipating. I grab it.

"Presents," Holly manages to say and I hold back a laugh.

"Or…" I give her a little tug and she falls on my chest, the thick comforter between us. "We could make everyone wait a little longer." Holly's face is above mine and her cheeks go pink, just like I hoped they would.

"Why are you naked?" Holly's question is so unexpected that I start laughing, shaking both of us.

"I'm not."

"But…"

"I pulled off the top of the onesie. This thing is like a million degrees."

"Oh." The pink on Holly's cheeks deepens.

"Presents?" I ask her, because as much fun as this is, teasing her, I don't want to push my luck.

Holly scrambles up from the bed. "Yes. Upstairs. Now." She turns away from me while I get out of the bed, and she doesn't look at me again until I've zipped up the pjs that make me feel like a hot pocket about to melt from the inside out. She holds my hand as I follow her up the stairs where there are now presents surrounding the tree and piled everywhere.

Tally and Noah are already awake, curled together on the floor in front of the couch.

"Merry Christmas," Tally says through a yawn as Holly leads me to another clear spot on the floor. I notice the presents are actually in little piles and I assume there is one for each of us.

"We all get presents?" I whisper to Holly as Gran comes in from the kitchen holding a steaming mug.

Holly gives me a weird look. "Of course."

"But they didn't know I was coming until last week."

Holly shrugs a bit. "Gran is a gift giver. She asked me what things I thought you might like and went shopping the other day. Did you really think you were going to not have any presents?"

I don't tell her that I never got presents growing up. That I was in foster homes too often with parents who didn't care enough to give the two teenage boys in their home any gifts other than underwear or socks. I've received presents here and there from the few friends I have, but for the most part, Christmas is just a normal day for me. A day where I sleep in and don't have to work.

Holly hands me a few packages that all have my name on them. "Merry Christmas," she says again before we all start opening our presents.

The gifts are hilarious—which I should have expected from knowing Gran for a week. She got me a few gag gifts, and hot pink socks 'for when you go running' she told me.

It shouldn't make me emotional, but I definitely can't find the words to share just how much it means to me.

"I had your present mailed to your house," I tell Holly. After we got back from our double date with Tally and Noah, I finally looked at the pictures that Noah had captured of us. My favorite one was taken after we had fallen in the snow—her hair had started to fall, but the way that we're looking at each other feels so genuine and happy—and I'm glad the moment was captured on camera. I had it printed on a canvas, and sent directly to Holly so she doesn't have to worry about taking it home on the airplane.

"Now I'm intrigued." She smiles up at me.

"Why didn't you just give it to her earlier?" Noah asks. "If you didn't bring it."

I shrug. "I kind of waited till the last minute and it didn't come in time. It'll be at her house when we get back."

Noah seems to accept this explanation, but I can feel Tally's eyes on me. I don't look at her though, I just keep looking at Holly.

Gran saves me from replying. "I've got one more big surprise for all of you."

She hands each one of us an envelope and her eyes are sparkling. Inside the envelope is a plane ticket with my name on it for next summer. To Maui.

"Gran," Holly says, as if this is too much. It is too much. They barely met me, and now they bought me a ticket to join them on what, a family vacation? It's too much.

Gran just waves her hand in the air. "It'll be a fun trip. Plus, Tally and Noah finally decided on their wedding date. It'll be a destination wedding, small of course. If they had their way, they'd elope, but I'm not letting that happen. It'll be us, and your father and Beth of course. And Noah's sister Annie and his friend Sam. Small and sweet and then we can still enjoy the beach."

"I don't know what to say," I say honestly.

"Just give me a hug and say thank you. We're happy to have you as part of the family now."

"Gran!" I glance at Holly as I'm getting up off the floor to hug Gran. Her cheeks are pink. "He's my boyfriend, not my fiancé."

Gran simply smiles as I give her a hug and she squeezes

me back. For once, I don't feel the immediate desire to pull away. Maybe having people who care about you isn't a bad thing.

"So?" Gran says. "It'll be a fun time."

Holly just shakes her head then looks at Tally. "I can't believe she talked you into a destination wedding."

"It wasn't that hard," Tally laughs. "Though, the book club ladies were kind of upset when we told them last week."

"And you didn't tell me!?" Holly narrows her eyes.

"Gran wanted the trip to be a surprise. So, we're telling you today."

Holly shakes her head but crawls over to her sister. "I'm so happy for you."

"Thanks, sis."

It's a heartwarming moment. One that makes me almost wish I had a better relationship with Leo. If things had gone down differently, maybe we would see each other for holidays and other times when family gets together. But I haven't seen him in almost four years. Not since he ran off with my fiancé.

I swallow the pain of that day. I'm happy right now and that's truly all that matters.

Tally has just asked me to tell my deepest darkest secret in our very mild game of truth or dare—no way was I picking dare after Gran made Noah run out in the snow barefoot—but I don't even know if I have a deepest darkest secret.

I'm saved from answering by my phone ringing in my pocket.

It's a number I don't recognize, which always makes my gut clench, but Leo has my number and even though I should probably block it, I haven't yet. So, it probably isn't him.

It probably isn't socially acceptable to answer your phone in the middle of a game, but I do it anyway. "Hello."

"Hello. Is this Andrew Rossi?" A female voice comes through on the other end.

"Yes." My gut seems to clench even harder. When a stranger calls and uses your full name, it's hardly ever a good sign.

"There's been an accident. You were listed as the emergency contact for Leo Rossi and his wife. They are both in surgery right now and the baby is in the NICU."

My mind isn't moving fast enough to process anything this woman is saying. But Holly, who's right by my side and surely heard every word, takes the phone from my frozen fingers.

"Hi, this is Holly. I'm Drew's girlfriend," I hear her say but the world starts to buzz around me.

An accident.

Leo.

Janessa.

A baby.

Reality crashes back down around me when I hear Holly say, "we'll be there as soon as we can."

She hands me back my phone and I stare at her blankly. "I'm not going," I tell her.

"Yes. We are." Holly is already looking at flights for today on her phone.

"I can't, Holly."

The look Holly gives me sends something straight through my heart. "After my mom was in her accident you don't think I did everything I could to make it in time. I didn't get to say good-bye, Drew. She died from her injuries while I was on my way to the airport. I'm not going to let that happen to you."

"But..."

"Bad blood or not, we're going." Holly's already up and

moving, looking down at her phone, as she heads to her room to pack her bag. She turns just before she gets out of the room. "I can get us on a flight in a few hours, we should get going."

I sit there frozen, completely aware that there are three sets of eyes on me.

"What's happening?" Noah finally asks.

"My brother," I say stiffly. I clear my throat. "He was in an accident with his wife. Apparently, I'm their emergency contact. But I haven't talked to either of them in four years. Not since she left me at the altar for him."

I think Tally gasps a little at that. If I was more aware of what was happening, I think this is the type of situation one would call ironic. But it's not really ironic. It's just sad. And annoying.

Like seriously? I'm finally having a good time. I'm moving on from the crap that happened all those years ago and I'm really falling for someone else for the first time—something I never thought would happen to me. And then this happens? My brother and his wife are in an accident and the person they call is me?

Deep down I know it makes sense. Janessa lived in one of the group homes Leo and I did when we were growing up. Leo and I had each other but she had no one, not until she and I started dating. Then she had me. And Leo.

I want to hold onto my bitterness. I don't want to rush to California to see how they're doing. I'm not ready to forgive them. But I don't think that I'm going to have much of a choice —at least with the not going part. I know Holly well enough now to know that she's going to make me get on that plane and then she'll probably drive me to the hospital herself.

But I'm not ready.

HOLLY

Rule #10: He won't walk away when things get hard.

DREW WAS quiet through rushed goodbyes and on the way to the airport, and he still is as we board the plane. He's subdued in a way that I've never seen him before, and I don't know if I'm making the right choice.

I pull out my phone to text Tally.

ME

> Am I making the right choice? Pushing him to see his brother?

Drew slumps in the seat next to me, staring out the window and I want to ask him what he's thinking about but my tongue feels like it weighs thirty pounds and is stuck in my mouth.

TALLY

> He should go. Even if he doesn't want to. I know there's history there (so much that I don't even know) but it's still his brother.

I nod, even though she can't see me and put my phone in airplane mode.

I get that Drew's brother hurt him and that his ex-fiancé hurt him too. I'm not asking him to forgive them. But they put him as their emergency contact and I feel like that means something.

Plus. There's a little baby who was born five weeks early whose parents are both in surgery. That baby needs someone too.

By the time we land in California, I've come up with a complete scenario about what's about to happen in my head. We'll go to the hospital to see Drew's brother, his wife, and the baby. If Drew's brother and his wife don't make it, Drew and I will get married right away and take care of the baby.

It's a huge leap. A jump in our brand-new relationship that I'm really not ready for, but I'd do it, just so the baby can have two parents who are married. I know that people don't have to be married to have kids, but call me old fashioned.

I'm about to tell Drew this fantastic plan I've come up with, just in case the worst truly does happen when he talks first.

"You don't have to come with me to the hospital," he says casually as he pulls his carryon from the compartment above us. "It might be better if I go alone."

I swallow thickly. In all of the scenarios I pictured in my head, I never took into account that Drew might not want me there with him. "If that's what you want."

Drew nods but I can tell that it's not the truth. There's no truth in his eyes. He doesn't want to do this at all, and for sure not alone. But he's pushing me away. "I just think it'll be better if I go alone."

I drive us back to our bungalows in silence, I have no idea what to say. I want Drew to change his mind and ask me to come with him. I won't invite myself along if he really doesn't want me there. By the time I pull into my driveway, Drew still hasn't said a word. "Do you need—" I start to say as Drew says "thanks for a great week."

I walk around the car and give him a tight hug. He hugs me back as if he's afraid to let go. In the end though, he steps back and before letting go he presses his lips against my forehead. He releases me and I head up my walkway alone. Drew lingers in his driveway and I'm tempted to watch through our peep hole to see if he actually leaves. But I don't. I shut the door behind me and sink to the ground wondering if I'll ever recover from this whirlwind of a week.

I feel like I now understand how easy it is to fall in love and how much it hurts at the same time.

Love? Can I really love Drew after just a week together? Is that even possible? Maybe what I feel isn't love exactly, or maybe it is. Maybe it's the beginning of something deep and real and beautiful and crazy and wild. Because isn't that what love is? Those moments you'd do absolutely anything for the other person just to make them smile or make them feel a little better.

Before I can stop myself, I run back out the door, but Drew's car—the one he rarely drives—is already gone.

I'm still standing there when the rain starts.

chapter 27

DREW

I'M SOAKED through to the skin by the time I get myself to walk through the hospital doors. Driving here was simple. But actually getting out of the car took me fifteen minutes. I have no idea how long I've been standing, watching people hurry in and out of the main doors, all I know is that my shoes squeak on the bright linoleum flooring as I make my way up to the front desk.

"Can I help you?" An older woman, probably in her sixties, smiles up at me.

"I'm here to see someone?" It comes out like a question, but the woman doesn't say anything. She just looks at her computer, ready to type.

"Leo Rossi." I bite my cheek after I say his name, hard enough that the coppery taste of blood fills my mouth. Am I actually doing this?

"He's out of surgery," the woman tells me. "But due to his injuries, he's going to be held in the ICU tonight. You're welcome to go up to his room, 407, until visiting hours end at eleven."

She hands me a sticker that says 'visitor' and tells me I need to go up to level four to get to his room, and the nurses on that level can answer any questions I have. I nod and stuff my hands into my jacket pocket. The elevator ride to the fourth floor takes what feels like ten minutes and I almost don't walk out when I get there. The doors open and I see a woman in scrubs whose hair looks like Holly's, and I step out.

She's the only reason I'm doing this. I'm no good for her if I can't put my past demons behind me. She deserves so much more than a man who has a closet full of skeletons and an anger-filled heart. Holly showed me this week what it was like to have a real family, to have people who genuinely care about you, without asking for anything in return. It was refreshing and incredible and I completely, stupidly, fell in love with Holly Nelson.

Which is why I had to come here alone. I don't trust myself to not get into a yelling match with my brother, even if he did just survive a car crash. And I know that would have killed Holly to see. But there are some things I want to say to Leo, and it is finally time to say them.

Well, when he wakes up.

I ask one of the nurses where room 407 is and she points down the hallway to the left. I make my way to his room, pausing with my hand on the door handle, and take a shaky breath before I open the door.

Leo is asleep on the bed, he's connected to several tubes and wires, but the machine to the right side of his bed tells me he's alive, maybe not well, but alive. "Damn it, Leo," I whisper as I shut the door behind me. He looks like crap—one of his arms is in a sling and the other has a cast.

I sink slowly into the chair beside his bed, looking at the one man who I always thought would be there for me. He has a few stitches along a cut across his forehead, and as he sleeps, it hits me just how young he looks. He always seemed so mature when we were growing up, but right now, lying in this hospital bed, he seems so young.

"I'm sorry I haven't been around," I whisper. The ache in my chest seems to loosen as they come free. "But you really hurt me. I met someone though, someone who's been showing me that maybe I've been holding onto my hurt and anger for a bit too long."

Leo shifts in the bed, but doesn't wake up. He'll still be coming out of anesthesia when he wakes up. He's only in the ICU because he lost so much blood, at least that's what the nurse at the desk told me.

"I'm not ready to be friends again," I whisper, knowing I'll have to have this conversation again when he's awake, but I need to get the words out now, or else I won't be able to then. "But I think I'm ready to forgive you."

I lean back in the chair, and the next thing I know, I'm being shaken awake by a nurse. "Sorry, sir, we didn't know you'd be staying. Can I get you a cot?"

Sleepy, I nod. "That'd be great." If I leave, I'm not coming back, so I've got to stay so I can talk to Leo.

The next morning, Leo is awake before I am. "They're moving me to a new room this morning," he tells me when I sit up on my cot. "Next to Janessa's." Before, when I heard her name, it felt like a knife straight to my heart, but today I don't feel a thing.

"I'm not ready to see her," I tell him.

Leo nods, slowly. "I didn't think you'd come."

"I didn't think I would either," I tell him honestly. "But I met someone."

Leo gives me a wry grin, one that makes my stomach clench

and I know that we have a long way to go before there will be any trust between us. "And she changed you?"

I nod. Not giving him any more than that. "I wanted to apologize." I swallow. Better now or never, right? "For holding onto all the anger for so long."

Leo watches me intently before he speaks. "I mean...I don't blame you; she was your fiancé."

"Yeah. But we were young, and we were the first people we'd ever loved, of course it wasn't going to last." I shake my head. "But it was still a bad move on your part."

"I take full responsibility for my actions," Leo says.

"I'm not ready to be friends," I tell him. Or real brothers, but saying that out loud feels like too much.

Leo gives me a sad smile. "I know."

"But I forgive you," I say. "And I'll stick around here for a few days to help out with the baby or whatever you need. But I'm not going to see Janessa."

"Understood," Leo says. "Thank you, Drew."

I duck my head a bit and slip on my shoes. "I'm going to see if this place has a gym and I'll be back once you get moved." I don't wait for Leo's reply.

Baby steps.

chapter 28

HOLLY

Rule #1: He needs to put me first.

"THAT'S THE THING TALLY, I don't think he wants to see me." I'm sitting in my room with my laptop on my lap as I look up all the galleries in my area that are accepting new artists right now. It's supposed to be distracting me from the whole Drew thing and the fact that we've been back home in California for five days and I haven't heard from him. His house has been dark too and his car hasn't been back—I've had Adrienne check so I could stop feeling so creepy—but the distractions aren't working.

"Have you reached out to him at all?" Tally's voice fills up my room since she's on speaker.

"Yes. I've texted him every day, only once though. I don't want to seem too annoying. I also tried calling twice, but it just goes straight to voicemail." Which means his phone is off and he doesn't want to talk to me—something that makes me want to spiral and binge watch a crime show, but I haven't hit that point yet. I do have several recommendations in my Netflix queue though, and if I don't hear from Drew in the next couple of days, I really might lose it.

Tally sighs. "But you really like him, right? Like at some point it became real instead of just pretend?"

We haven't talked about it yet, she and I. I have been trying to sort through my own feelings while also ignoring the fact that Drew left and didn't ask me to come with him and I have no clue what's happening. *Don't spiral, Holly.* I tell myself before responding to Tally. "Yes. It was real at the end. He told me he wanted to see where things went with us and now, I've been ghosted."

"You haven't been ghosted," Tally says and I know she's just trying to make me feel better, but it's not working. I've been ghosted. "His brother was just in an accident and was having major surgery, and it's the first time he's seen him in four years after what happened. Give him time. But really sis, I'm proud of you. Letting go of all your rules."

I hold back a smile. I don't know if I'll ever admit it, but I'm kind of proud too. "He showed me that love and romance were different from movies and in a good way. What I wanted was a fantasy, what I might have is the real thing. But that doesn't change the fact that he didn't want me there with him through this hard thing."

"He didn't ghost you," Tally says again.

"You didn't see the look he gave me when he told me that he didn't want me to come with him. He checked out. He's done." I leave out the hug that he gave me before he left. I may be wrong, but it kind of felt like a goodbye hug.

"You don't know that until he actually says that," Tally tells me. And logically, that makes sense, but something in my gut tells me that he's done. I moved too fast and freaked him out.

"Yeah, if he ever talks to me again."

My phone chimes, I lunge for it. It's only a text from Jim.

JIM SULLIVAN

I'm free this afternoon, if that works for you.

I know I should feel dread in my belly about what I'm about to do, but this is the only thing that's actually made me feel calm in the past five days.

ME

That works great. How about two?

JIM SULLIVAN

Two is fine.

"Holly? You still there?" Tally asks and I realize I completely missed if she said something or not before that.

"Yup. I'm here. Just planning my meet up with Jim later."

"Do you really think it's a good idea?" Tally asks me, but I'm not going to let her talk me out of this.

"It's time, Tally. I have to do this."

"Okay."

"Okay. Now can I go? I need to finish up some things before I see Jim. And I need to see if Drew is home."

"Just call him again!" Tally says. "Or go to the hospital to see him. He probably could use a friend right now."

But I know now that I don't want to just be his friend. I want more. "I know. I'll go. Tomorrow, if I don't talk to him by then."

"Chicken."

"I'm hanging up now."

"I get that you don't want to get hurt, but doesn't not knowing what he's actually thinking hurt more?" Tally asks me softly.

"I'm not answering that question," I say and then hang up the phone. I can do this. If everything goes alright today, it'll be easier to see Drew and tell him what my plans for the future are, then no matter what he says, everything will be fine.

DREW

I'M WAITING in Leo's hospital room for him to come back from his physical therapy when there's a knock on the door before it swings open.

For the half a second between the knock and when I see him, I hope it's Holly. I know I shouldn't be ignoring her calls and texts; I just don't know what to tell her.

But it's Jim.

"Hey man," Jim gives me an awkward wave. "Holly said this is where I'd find you."

A million emotions hit me in the gut. Holly and Jim are talking now? She sent him here? I've been trying to figure out my own feelings and she's talking to another man?

I swallow. I can still be Jim's friend. "Hey."

"How are you doing?" Jim asks me. "How's your brother and his wife?"

"I'm okay." That's a lie. I'm falling apart. My entire world got flipped around in less than two weeks. I fell for a truly fantastic woman—something I'm barely able to admit to myself —and I somewhat reconciled with my brother. How am I supposed to be doing? "And Leo's going to be fine. His wife has

a longer road to recover, her legs were both crushed in the accident. But she'll be okay, and their baby is doing well too. He's a
fighter."

"Good." Jim nods like all of this makes sense. I want to ask
him about Holly, if he's seen her—why he's seen her even
though I know she turned him down for that New Year's Eve
party, at least that's what she told me. "I brought some Chinese
food." He holds up a bag. "I'm about to go have a late lunch with
Holly, but I thought you might be sick of the cafeteria food."

"Thanks for coming, man." I get the words out, but I don't
actually mean them. I want to ask why he's going out to lunch
with Holly, but he doesn't know that I've fallen for her.

"Of course. You bringing me takeout when my housemate
was in the hospital was a life saver. Just returning the favor." Jim
sets the bag of food on the little table beside me. My stomach
rolls at the smell—or the fact that I'm playing nice with the man
who's about to take my woman out on a date.

"Thanks," I say again.

"Well, I can't stay long. Just wanted to drop this by," Jim
says. He's been awkwardly standing the whole time, and for one
earth-shattering moment, I wonder what it is that Holly sees in
him. I guess she sees enough that even after the past week
together, she's brave enough to give him a chance. "I'll see you
next week at the faculty meeting."

I manage to wave goodbye. As soon as he's out of the room,
I'm drafting a text to Holly.

ME

> Are you really going to give up on me that
> easily? There's been a lot going on and I've
> needed to process it all, I thought you would
> get that. But you're going out with Jim?

I don't send it. It sounds childish and like I'm a jealous

boyfriend, but I'm not her boyfriend, we never had that talk. I delete the whole thing and turn off my phone.

My stomach growls so I reach in the bag for the takeout. I pull out the fortune first. "Holly really made you a rebel, huh," I say as I crack it open and slide the little paper out.

A romantic endeavor will bring you love.

"Ha, that's a load of crap." I take the uneaten fortune cookie, and the rest of the food and step into the hallway. I toss everything in the nearest garbage can and head back to Leo's room.

"What's that face for?" Leo asks me when he returns to his room. He's got a broken arm and a shoulder that needed surgery, but other than that he's okay.

"What face?" I nearly growl. I'm in a bad mood. I've been nothing but upbeat and putting on a good front since I've been here, but the fact that Holly is going out with another man has me hitting my limit.

"You look like someone just told you that your dog died."

"I don't like dogs."

"No, you don't like pets, there's a big difference," Leo laughs and I know he's trying to lighten the mood, but it isn't going to work.

"Whatever."

"Drew."

I look at him. We've come a long way over the past few days, but we're still not close. We're still not friends. The only reason I'm still here is because Janessa had another surgery today, but tomorrow I'm going home.

"What happened?"

"Nothing," I tell him. I haven't told him much about Holly. It's not that I don't trust him—which I don't, not completely—

but the last time I loved a woman, he married her so I'm not exactly risking anything. Even if she is about to go out with another man, a man who I thought was my friend. I clench my fists so hard my nails dig into my palms.

"Take a walk," Leo says as he sits down on his bed. "Cool down from whatever it is that made you mad. They're bringing Jonah down in a little bit so we can see him. Janessa might come too."

I nod and stand, fresh air will probably do me some good. I haven't been outside in at least four days. I also haven't seen Janessa yet.

Leo's betrayal hurt more than hers, but I'm not ready to talk to her yet. They both seem to understand. But whenever it's baby visiting time, I head to the cafeteria or walk the halls until she goes back to her room.

As I make my way outside, the Southern California sun hits my face. I turn left and start running. My legs protest immediately. That's what happens when you run nearly every day for years and then suddenly take a week off. But I just push myself harder, the sound of my feet hitting the pavement slows something in my mind for the first time since I went to Utah. By the time I make it back to the hospital—four miles later—I'm more mad than I was before.

She was supposed to be mine, I thought she fell for me? And like a fool, I fell for her, when it was never real for her to begin with.

 *chapter 30*

DREW

I'M DOZING on the uncomfortable cot that's pushed against one of the walls in Leo's room when there's a quiet knock on the door, pulling me from my nap. Leo doesn't move or even wake up. There's no such thing as a good night's sleep when you're at a hospital, not with the nurses coming to check Leo's vitals every couple of hours.

I could go home, but now I just feel ashamed from hiding so long from Holly that I don't know what I'll do when I face her again.

"Excuse me," a nurse calls from the doorway. "But there's someone here to see you."

"Aren't visiting hours over?" I whisper loudly over Leo's deep snores.

"Yes, but tonight we made an exception," the nurse whispers back. I roll on my side and lift my hand to wake Leo up. I have no idea who on earth would be here to see him. I don't even know who he's told that he's here besides a few guys at work. "Don't wake him. The visitor is for you."

I glance at the nurse whose face is dark because of the bright hall lights behind her. I give her a curious glance but head out.

Standing by the nurse's station is Holly. She's wearing a long silver skirt that seems to shine under the fluorescent lights and a sweater that says 'Make art, not goals.'

My heart does a flip.

"Hi." Holly gives me a little wave.

I hold back the urge to pull her into my arms. My entire body seems to relax just at the sight of her, and I know now I was wrong in not letting her come here with me. And now I've pushed her away, into the arms of someone else.

"Walk with me?" she asks, holding out a hand. I take it as she pulls me toward the elevators. But instead of going down like I assume, she hits the top floor.

"Where are we going?"

"You'll see," Holly says. She doesn't ask me how I'm doing. She doesn't tell me about her date with Jim today. We simply stand there listening to the hospital elevator music as we go up to the top floor.

The door pings and opens when we reach it and Holly pulls me out. There are a few nurses in hats and holding cups who smile at us. I follow Holly along a narrow hallow that ends at a door. "You ready for this?"

"For what, exactly?" I ask her. Holly pushes open the door and the cool night air hits my face.

"For a firework show." We walk onto a terrace that covers the roof of the hospital. There are a few tables and chairs along with potted plants.

"How did you know this was up here?" I ask her, following her to the edge where to our left is nothing but dark ocean and to our right is our city.

"I came up here a lot when I brought Adrienne for physical therapy after she broke her wrist two years ago. There wasn't really any point in me dropping her off and going home since I was her ride and the appointments weren't that long, so

I found this place. Well, actually a nice nurse told me about it."

"Wow."

"How are you doing?" Holly asks. She still hasn't dropped my hand and I look at her fingers tangled with mine.

"I'm...feeling a million little things," I tell her honestly.

She looks out toward the beach where they set off fireworks every year at midnight, the only part of town that actually allows it. "Understandable."

"Are you mad I didn't text?" I ask her.

Holly looks at me curiously. "Why would I be mad? Mad isn't the right word for it. Worried? Yes. Nervous that you decided to ghost me because falling for someone in just six days is really fast? Also, yes. But in the end Tally talked me down, at least mostly. I tried to give you space but also let you know that I was here for you."

"Thank you," I tell her. "I wish I hadn't pushed you away."

Holly flips her hair over her shoulder and gives me what I think is supposed to be a smug smile, but she just looks adorable. "Well thanks. I can be here whenever you need me to be."

"Can you though?" I ask her and she tilts her head in confusion. "I know you went out with Jim today."

"Gosh dang it. That man nearly ruined my surprise." Those words don't really make me feel any better.

"Your surprise?"

"Yes. This is the part of every rom-com ever where I come to you, even though you walked away, so really the grand gesture should be your job, but I couldn't wait anymore, so I came to convince you that we're right for each other. That my dumb list of rules doesn't actually matter. That I think you are the guy that's perfect for me, right now. And to tell you that just because you've never had this kind of love before, doesn't mean you don't deserve it and doesn't mean you need to push it away."

My mind is struggling to catch up, but Holly keeps talking.

"And yeah. I just said the "l" word and you know, I don't know if I'm there yet but maybe I am because I do fall hard and fast for men I've never even talked to, so of course I'd fall for you after we spent a week together. But it wasn't just you being there that made me fall for you. It was the way you beat me in my own contest with graham cracker houses. And when you took care of me when I was sick. And when you kissed me for real, I knew you felt it too. I've been falling for you since we got on that airplane to fly to Utah, and all I really know is that you make life better. You encourage me to chase my dreams in a way that makes me actually believe that what I want isn't just a dream, but something that could be a reality."

"I—" I start to say, my heart beating wildly in my chest.

Holly holds up the hand that's not holding mine. "I have more. Please let me finish."

I nod. "Okay."

Holly smiles. "I didn't go out with Jim like you're thinking. It was just a quick meeting where I told him that he should start looking for a replacement art teacher because I'm done at the end of this year. I've been submitting my art to different galleries since we got back and I already applied to teach an adult art class at one of them. You gave me the courage to do that."

"Holly, that's amazing!" I pick her up and give her a twirl, this time though we don't slip and fall to the ground.

"Yeah?" Holly asks.

"Yes." I hear a firework go off in the distance, part of my brain starts to question why on earth people are lighting off fireworks *today* when it's not even New Year's Eve yet, but instead I pull Holly closer to me. "I'm falling in love with you too."

Holly smiles up at me. "And I'm sorry I didn't reach out sooner. I forgave my brother and then felt like I should stay to help him while Janessa is still recovering and in multiple surg-eries. But I'm coming home tomorrow."

"Good," Holly says. "I've missed you."

"It's been like five days, that's like half of our relationship," I say, teasing her.

Holly hits my chest. "So? I was worried."

I press my forehead against hers. "I'm sorry I worried you. I'm kind of a newbie when it comes to relationships."

"Me too," Holly says. "Oh, that reminds me." She pulls out of my arms and grabs a folded piece of paper from her back pocket. "I want you to take this. You can rip it up or burn it or whatever, but I don't need it anymore. You were right, that man I had an idea of on paper doesn't exist."

I take the paper from her. "I think I'll start by teasing you about all the ways I'm different from your dream guy."

Holly smacks my chest again. "Do not. You're better than any guy I could have imagined."

"I mean, I guess I'll have to shave my beard." I rub it thoughtfully.

"Do not," Holly says. "I love it."

"You'd better." I grin at her and then I kiss her.

 *epilogue*

SIX MONTHS LATER – HOLLY

I'm practically bouncing as I make my way from the studio into my small, makeshift office at the gallery I got a job at three weeks ago. Just like I promised, I finished out the school year at the high school, then moved on to something different.

"Hey." Drew smiles at me as he walks through the door. "You had a full house out there!"

I nod, not trusting myself to open my mouth yet. I can't believe I just did that.

The first teaching job I applied for at a studio was turned down, as was my art at pretty much every gallery in town. I was trying to be brave and put my art out there. I used all of my old stuff, not quite ready to commit to the style that Drew seemed to unlock in me over Christmas break.

Once a week though—since Christmas—he took me to a private studio where we'd paint together, and over the past few months, I finally let my guard down and gave into creating the art that I really want to create, instead of what I think other people might like.

Two weeks ago, I signed on with a newer gallery who wants to showcase my pieces starting next week for the whole summer.

While my art is here, I get an office and two nights a week I get to teach adults how to make art. Art that comes from their souls.

"Was that even real?" I ask. I can hardly believe that this is my life now, that I get to spend my days creating art and then teaching others to do the same. Tonight, I was in a room full of people, and instead of feeling alone, I felt alive.

Drew pulls me against his chest. "It was real. This is real."

I let out an incredulous laugh.

"You did amazing." Drew steps back from me. "And I know I told you we'd go out to celebrate your first day, but before we head out, I need you to come with me."

Drew threads his fingers through mine and tugs me toward the small staircase at the back of the gallery that leads up to a private studio.

We're greeted by hundreds of tiny glowing candles that cover the floor. "Isn't this a fire hazard?"

"They're fake," Drew says and then he kneels in front of me. My mouth opens in surprise. "Holly Nelson, when I begged you to let me come home with you for Christmas six months ago, I never expected to fall in love with you. But I did and I fall in love with you more each day. I love your heart and your passion and your joy. I know we've kind of been dating for the past six months, but I think it's time to make it official. Will you be my girlfriend?"

I roll my eyes and give his shoulder a playful shove. "I've been your girlfriend for six months, you dingus."

"Well then." Drew's eyes are gleaming now. "What do you say about being my wife?"

My mouth drops open into a perfect o. I've dreamed of this moment for at least half my life, but once Drew came along and I fell for him, I became content with taking it slow, simply because Drew isn't a fan of marriage. Being with him has been enough.

Drew looks up at me and the skin around his eyes wrinkles as he smiles. "I love you, Nelson. I want to marry you. You showed me that love could be so much more than I ever imagined." Drew chuckles. "Bet you didn't think I'd say those words any time soon."

I shake my head.

Drew holds up a simple ring. It's a gold band with tiny diamonds all around it. "Marry me?" He asks again.

"Yes!" I pull him up to me. Drew kisses me deeply and then pulls away.

"How about next month? A double wedding with Tally and Noah," Drew says as he slips the ring on my finger.

"How about we don't overshadow their moment and have our own. I'm thinking... the week of Christmas, maybe before my birthday."

Drew smiles at me. "That's perfect."

"But you have to wear a gray suit. That's my only rule."

Drew presses a gentle kiss against my forehead. "You and your rules."

I smack his arm.

"But I think I can manage a gray suit."

THE END

RULES FOR MY FUTURE HUSBAND BY HOLLY NELSON

1. He needs to put me first
2. My future husband will never have a beard because they don't look good on anyone
3. He always opens doors for me
4. He has to have a cute smile :)
5. Tattoos are okay, just no exes names
6. He has to lean (like in While You Were Sleeping)
7. No kissing on the first date—doesn't believe in kissing on the first date
8. He has a good relationship with his mom
9. My future husband and I will have a meet-cute. We'll actually like each other right from the start, not like in Harry Met Sally.
10. He won't walk away when things get hard.
11. He loves watching romcoms and thrillers (because I have excellent taste in movies across a variety of genres)
12. Likes going on walks

13. Likes to be goofy / is funny / happy

14. He has goals for the future

15. We have to be friends at least 6 months before we begin dating

16. He has to care deeply about life, other people, and me

17. He has to appreciate art

18. He has to love Christmas

19. He has to like good food. Can also cook, maybe?

20. Is romantic <3

21. He has to have blue eyes

ACKNOWLEDGMENTS

Wow. Here we are again. I'd hoped that this would be easier the second time around, but it doesn't seem to be any easier.

First, like last time, I am so thankful to God for His unwavering support and guidance throughout this process.

Second, a huge thank you to all of my early readers! My sister, McKenna, and my aunt Sara read the very first draft of this book back in 2021, and without their support and encouragement I don't think it would be in your hands today.

Thank you to my beta readers, Meaghan and Ashley, and to my editor Kristen. You helped make this book better. Thank you for your endless love and encouragement and edits. This book is what it is today because of you.

And, this book is so special because I tried to put in some of my own Christmas traditions in these pages. So to both sets of grandparents, all of my aunts and uncles, and my cousins, thank you for giving me all these Christmas memories that make me feel like Holly at times. I don't want to grow up sometimes because our childhood was so magical.

To my parents, thank you for supporting me and reading my books. I love you both. And thank you Dad, for helping out with the title on this one (which was almost called A Boyfriend for Christmas), but we liked The Rules of Mistletoe better.

To Griffin and Von. I love you both to the moon and back. You light up my life every single day.

And to you dear reader, thank you thank you thank for

being here. For reading this romance and talking about it. You mean the world to mean!

ABOUT THE AUTHOR

Taylor Epperson has dreamed of writing books since she was a kid. She firmly believes that every story needs kissing and romance. Her stories will make you swoon, laugh, and maybe cry. But hopefully they'll always leave you feeling a little happier.

When she's not writing, you can find her curled up with a good book and a bag of potato chips or playing with her daughter. She enjoys binge-watching cooking shows and crime dramas. She lives in Northern Colorado with her husband, daughter, and very anxious black lab.

Sign up for Taylor's newsletter to get all the info about her next release: https://authortaylorepperson.substack.com/

Made in the USA
Middletown, DE
27 October 2023

41371660R00123